I0591872

# Over the Moon

by Steven Dietz

Adapted from *The Small Bachelor*
by P.G. Wodehouse

## FOR PRODUCTION INQUIRIES

### UNITED STATES AND CANADA
info@concordtheatricals.com
1-866-979-0447

### UNITED KINGDOM AND EUROPE
licensing@concordtheatricals.co.uk
020-7054-7298

Each title is subject to availability from Concord Theatricals Corp.,
depending upon country of performance. Please be aware that *OVER
THE MOON* may not be licensed by Concord Theatricals Corp. in
your territory. Professional and amateur producers should contact the
nearest Concord Theatricals Corp. office or licensing partner to verify
availability.

No one shall make any changes in this title(s) for the purpose of production. No part of this book may be reproduced, stored in a retrieval system, scanned, uploaded, or transmitted in any form, by any means, now known or yet to be invented, including mechanical, electronic, digital, photocopying, recording, videotaping, or otherwise, without the prior written permission of the publisher. No one shall share this title(s), or any part of this title(s), through any social media or file hosting websites.

For all inquiries regarding motion picture, television, online/digital and other media rights, please contact Concord Theatricals Corp.

## MUSIC AND THIRD-PARTY MATERIALS USE NOTE

Licensees are solely responsible for obtaining formal written permission from copyright owners to use copyrighted music and/or other copyrighted third-party materials (e.g. artworks, logos) in the performance of this play and are strongly cautioned to do so. If no such permission is obtained by the licensee, then the licensee must use only original music and materials that the licensee owns and controls. Licensees are solely responsible and liable for clearances of all third-party copyrighted materials, including without limitation music, and shall indemnify the copyright owners of the play(s) and their licensing agent, Concord Theatricals Corp., against any costs, expenses, losses and liabilities arising from the use of such copyrighted third-party materials by licensees. For music, please contact the appropriate music licensing authority in your territory for the rights to any incidental music.

## IMPORTANT BILLING AND CREDIT REQUIREMENTS

If you have obtained performance rights to this title, please refer to your licensing agreement for important billing and credit requirements.

OVER THE MOON received its world premiere at the Arizona Theatre Company in Tucson AZ, on October 3rd, 2003. David Ira Goldstein, Artistic Director; Jessica L. Andrews, Managing Director. This production was co-produced with the Seattle Repertory Theatre, where it opened on November 13th, 2003. The director was David Ira Goldstein; scenic designer was Scott Weldin; costume designer was David Kay Mickelsen; lighting designer was John McLain; composer was Roberta Carlson; sound designer was Brian Jerome Peterson; dramaturg was Jennifer Lee Carrell; stage manager was Glenn Bruner. The cast was as follows:

GEORGE FINCH .............................. R. Hamilton Wright

HAMILTON BEAMISH............................... Bob Sorenson

MRS. WADDINGTON ................................... Suzy Hunt

SIGSBEE WADDINGTON ............................... Ken Ruta

MOLLY WADDINGTON ............................ Liz McCarthy

FERRIS............................................. David Pichette

MULLETT ...................................... Roberto Guajardo

FANNY WELCH ................................... Julie Briskman

GARROWAY.......................................... Jeff Steitzer

MADAME EULALIE ................................. Kirsten Potter

# CHARACTERS

**GEORGE FINCH** – (a lifelong bachelor)

"He is an artist. And what is more, probably the worst artist who ever put brush to canvas."

**HAMILTON BEAMISH** – (Finch's well-known friend)

"He knew everything there was to be known – or behaved as if he did – by the age of ten."

**MRS. WADDINGTON** – (a wealthy woman)

"I am loath to speak ill of a woman, but Mrs. Waddington is a bounder and a snob and has a soul like the under-side of a stone."

**SIGSBEE WADDINGTON** – (her husband)

"Many good judges considered that he had a head of concrete, but nobody had ever disparaged his heart."

**MOLLY WADDINGTON** – (their daughter)

"In addition to being a nice, dutiful girl, Molly Waddington was also a persuasive, wheedling girl."

**FERRIS** – (their butler, British)

"To the dramatist, the butler is indispensable."

**MULLETT** – (Finch's valet, a reformed thief)

"He looked like a man who had a favorite aunt in Poughkeepsie, and was always worried about her asthma."

**FANNY WELCH** – (Mullet's girlfriend, a pickpocket)

"One of the great advantages of being a pickpocket is that you do have nice hands."

**GARROWAY** – (a policeman and aspiring poet)

"He was a long, stringy policeman, who flowed out of his uniform at odd spots."

**MADAME EULALIE** – (a creative young woman)

"She was a girl of *chic* and *élan*. One may go still further – a girl of *espieglerie* and *je ne sais quoi*."

## SETTING

New York City.

The primary action of the play takes place on the roof of George Finch's apartment building in Sheridan Square. There are four ways to access the roof: from Finch's adjacent apartment (stage right); from his sleeping porch (stage left); from a covered stairwell (up right center); and from a fire escape (up left center). All but the sleeping porch provide a way to go "downstairs" and leave the building. Other locales should be designated with a minimum of objects, as noted. Action should be continuous.

## TIME

1927.

*"The moon, to really express itself,
needs the great open spaces."*

*P. G. Wodehouse*

# ACT ONE

## The Roof. Day.

(**MULLETT** *is sweeping with a broom, happily humming a little tune.* **BEAMISH** *emerges from the stairwell, and walks up directly behind him.*)

**BEAMISH.** Wrong-wrong-wrong-wrong-wrong!

(**MULLETT** *nearly jumps out of his shoes.*)

**MULLETT.** Sir!

**BEAMISH.** The angle of the arm. The sweep of the shoulder. The twist of the wrist. All wrong-wrong-wrong.

(*He hands* **MULLETT** *a small booklet.*)

Here. Read this.

**MULLETT.** "Techniques of Efficient Sweeping."

**BEAMISH.** A booklet for the modern broomstick operator.

**MULLETT.** Thank you, Mister Beamish.

**BEAMISH.** Improve Yourself, Mullett! That must be the goal of each and every one of us. America is hungry for self-improvement and the Beamish Booklets aim to do just that. Is there a policeman about?

**MULLETT.** Did you say a *policeman?*

**BEAMISH.** I said it and meant it.

**MULLETT.** Were you expecting one?

**BEAMISH.** I was and I am.

**MULLETT.** And what would a policeman be wanting up here on this roof?

**BEAMISH.** To become a poet, naturally. Don't they all?

**MULLETT.** Sir?

*(He hands* **MULLETT** *another booklet.)*

**BEAMISH.** I can make a poet out of anyone. With proper attention to that booklet, I could make a poet out of *two sticks and an orange peel.*

*(**BEAMISH** moves to the edge of the roof.)*

Our policeman will stand here on this roof, he will ingest the restless, teeming urban cacophony – and he will *poeticize it.*

**MULLETT.** And how long will that take?

**BEAMISH.** Till he's a poet?

**MULLETT.** Yes, sir.

**BEAMISH.** Three weeks, tops. Where's Mister Finch?

**MULLETT.** Gone to look at a young lady.

**BEAMISH.** You mean he's gone to *see her?*

**MULLETT.** No, sir. Only to look. You see, lately Mister Finch has been getting persnickety about his clothes –

**BEAMISH.** *Persnickety?*

**MULLETT.** Particular, sir.

**BEAMISH.** Then, *say* "particular", Mullet. Avoid jargon. Strive for the "Word Beautiful."

*(Another booklet.)*

**MULLETT.** Okeydoke.

*(Quick glance at the booklet.)*

I mean: *certainly.*

**BEAMISH.** Very good, Mullet. Now, go on.

**MULLETT.** Well, the last week or so, Mister Finch can't make up his mind about the ties.

**BEAMISH.** The ties.

**MULLETT.** I lay out the blue one with the pink twill – and he puts it on – and steps out the door – and then rushes back in, demanding the dove-grey with the burgundy crest.

**BEAMISH.** Very odd.

**MULLETT.** You can say that again.

**BEAMISH.** I can and I won't.

**MULLETT.** So, I *followed him* –

**BEAMISH.** Good for you, Mullet!

**MULLETT.** – all the way to East Seventy-Ninth Street.

**BEAMISH.** A splendid neighborhood.

**MULLETT.** And there he stopped and stood outside a very nice building. Watching a young lady come and go.

**BEAMISH.** Did he ever approach her?

**MULLETT.** Never once. And right then, I said to myself: HOT DOG!

**BEAMISH.** Mullett?

**MULLETT.** Sir?

**BEAMISH.** Please never use that revolting expression again.

**MULLETT.** Which one?

**BEAMISH.** *(Grits his teeth.)* The one about the...*small heated roll of meat.*

*(Another booklet.)*

**BEAMISH.** Take this, Mullett. Place it prominently on Mister Finch's dressing table.

**MULLETT.** *(Reads.)* "The Principles of Rational Matrimony."

**BEAMISH.** In that booklet I argue very strongly against love at first sight. The mating of the sexes should be a logical process – ruled by Reason and Intellect.

(**GARROWAY** *enters, and immediately –)*

(**MULLETT**'s *face goes ashen.)*

Garroway, there you are.

**GARROWAY.** I was detained at the Station House. We are planning a *very big raid* –

*(Re:* **MULLETT.**)

Wait. I know this man.

**BEAMISH.** This is Mullett. He works for my friend, George Finch.

**GARROWAY.** Your face, sir, looks very familiar.

**MULLETT.** I have that kind of face. I look just like everybody.

**BEAMISH.** Every*one*, Mullett.

**GARROWAY.** *(To* **MULLETT.**) Are you sure I haven't seen your *photograph somewhere?*

(**MULLETT** *moves away, shielding his face, as –)*

(**BEAMISH** *leads* **GARROWAY** *to the edge of the roof, indicates the view.)*

**BEAMISH**. Garroway, I want you to remove the Eyes of the Policeman and observe the world with the Eyes of the Poet.

> (**GARROWAY** *nods, takes off his policeman's hat – and puts a brightly colored beret on his head.*)

Now: tell me what you see.

**GARROWAY**. Well, way down there I see the "Purple Chicken" – one of these days that joint is going to get pinched!

> (*Whispers.*)

It's come to our attention that the Purple Chicken, in defiance of the Eighteenth Amendment, continues to serve *alcoholic beverages*.

**BEAMISH**. You mean a person can *get it* there.

**GARROWAY**. *They're* the ones who are going to *get it*. Me and boys are gonna pull off the biggest raid you ever saw!

**BEAMISH**. Garroway: a poet must learn the principles of Observation – not *Surveillance!* Now. This vista...this *paysage de urbain*: how does it strike you?

> (**GARROWAY** *studies the view.*)

**GARROWAY**. It looks...pretty.

**BEAMISH**. *Pretty?*

**GARROWAY**. No, I'm sorry: it looks...*very* pretty.

**BEAMISH**. I must tell you, Garroway, that the modern poet does not go around finding things "pretty."

**GARROWAY**. I see.

**BEAMISH**. It isn't "pretty" in the least.

**GARROWAY.**  No, sir?

**BEAMISH.**  It is *stark*.

**GARROWAY.**  "Stark," sir?

**BEAMISH.**  *Stark and grim*. It makes your heart ache. You see through the dirty windows – the torn and tattered blinds – and there you glimpse the broken dreams of each cowering soul trapped within. Their sorrow; their suffering; their sordid and eternal gloom.

> (**GARROWAY** *is staring, intently.*)

Don't you, Garroway?

> (**GARROWAY** *nods – nearly crying at the sight of it.*)

Now: take out your notebook and begin. I must find Mister Finch.

> (**BEAMISH** *leaves.*)

> (**GARROWAY** *moves away, and takes out his notebook, as –*)

> (**FINCH** *enters from the stairwell. He is carrying what appears to have once been his hat.*)

**FINCH.**  Mullet, take this hat.

**MULLETT.**  Shall I throw it away, sir?

**FINCH.**  Heavens, no! Wrap it in *white silk* – tenderly, as you would swaddle an infant in your arms – then leave it on the table in my sitting room. Perhaps with a flower near it. A white rose...in a delicate vase...the morning sun falling in upon it...

> (**FINCH** *has a far away look.* **MULLETT** *extends his hand, awaiting the hat.*)

**MULLETT.** Very good, sir.

>    (**FINCH** *hands the hat to* **MULLETT** – *who takes it and leaves.*)

>    (**FINCH** *steps to the edge of the roof and announces:*)

**FINCH.** Good people of New York! My name is George Finch! And I...AM...IN...

**GARROWAY.** Danger, sir.

**FINCH.** (*Turns, startled.*) Who are you?

**GARROWAY.** Name's Garroway. And I'm afraid I've got a rather disagreeable duty to perform. Your valet, Mister Mullett –

**FINCH.** What about him?

**GARROWAY.** I knew I'd seen his face. His photo was on the wall at the Station. He's a *thief.* Spent a year in prison for burglary. He was released only a month ago.

**FINCH.** During which time he has worked for me.

**GARROWAY.** Sorry, sir. Just thought you should know.

>    (**GARROWAY** *leaves, passing* **MULLETT**.)

Say, Mullett – weren't you at Sing Sing with a fella named "Joe the Gorilla"?

**MULLETT.** Big guy, one eyebrow, hands like giant hams?

**GARROWAY.** That's him.

**MULLETT.** Don't ring a bell.

>    (**GARROWAY** *gives* **FINCH** *a quick look, and is gone.*)

**FINCH.** Well, Mullett. This is rather unfortunate.

**MULLETT.** Most unpleasant, sir.

**FINCH.** Tell me: how did you – what was your –

**MULLETT.** My gambit?

**FINCH.** Yes. Your *gambit.*

**MULLETT.** I would get a job as a valet. Gain my employer's trust. And then skin out with everything I could lay my hands on.

**FINCH.** I can't believe this! Day after day, I have left my most valuable possessions in your care –

**MULLETT.** Oh, sir, those pearl studs! What a temptation – just sitting there in the drawer!

**FINCH.** I can imagine.

**MULLETT.** The Voice of the Tempter would call to me: "DO IT, MULLETT! NAB 'EM WHILE YOU CAN! WHAT ARE YOU WAITING FOR?!"

**FINCH.** Must have been very hard.

**MULLETT.** And when you were asleep, Mister Finch – oh, you should have heard the Tempter then! "SLIP A SPONGE OF CHLOROFORM UNDER HIS NOSE AND CLEAR OUT WITH THE SWAG!"

**FINCH.** All right – that's enough! Pack your bags.

**MULLETT.** But, sir, I'm reformed.

**FINCH.** *Religion*, I suppose?

**MULLETT.** Oh, no, sir: *love.*

**FINCH.** Love, Mullett?

**MULLETT.** If only you knew my Fanny.

**FINCH.** Yes, well, I –

**MULLETT.** She is the moon and the stars to me. I would do anything to give her the life she deserves.

**FINCH.** I see. You promised her you'd go straight.

**MULLETT.** Yes, sir. And one day I hope she'll do the same.

(*Off* **FINCH**'s *look.*)

She's a pickpocket. Finest in the city. She can take your watch from your pocket as she waves to you from across the street.

**FINCH.** That's quite impressive.

**MULLETT.** But the greatest thing she's stolen, sir, is my heart.

(**FINCH** *considers this.*)

**FINCH.** I've been *following someone*, Mullett. Have you ever done that?

**MULLETT.** No, sir.

**FINCH.** Well, this someone is a young woman who lives on East Seventy-Ninth Street.

**MULLETT.** Near the park.

**FINCH.** Have you been there?

**MULLETT.** No, sir.

**FINCH.** I've been watching her come and go. Once I saw her walking with a woman who seemed to be the horrid ghost of Catherine the Great.

**MULLETT.** Her mother, no doubt.

**FINCH.** Have you seen her?

**MULLETT.** No, sir.

**FINCH.** Anyway, I had never spoken to the young lady... until today. I was outside her house in my normal hiding place – when she came past me, walking a Scotch terrier on a leash. At that very moment, a gust of wind blew my hat off my head, and it was about to blow across the street when this lovely young lady STOMPED ON IT – stopping it, brilliantly! – whereupon the Scotch terrier took off like a bounder in the general direction of Brooklyn, with my hat in his teeth! I went in pursuit, of course, and when I restored him to his mistress, she looked in my eyes, Mullett – and, well, truth be told, I started to *choke and turn pink and twist my fingers and make funny noises through my nose* – but finally, *I did* manage to speak to her. I said: *"Here is your dog."*

**FINCH.** And then, in a voice filled with angels and songbirds and the music of the spheres, she said:

*"You have mud on your nose."*

Isn't that remarkable?!

**MULLETT.** What will you do, sir?

**FINCH.** I shall *dress,* Mullett! I shall dress *very carefully.*

**MULLETT.** Very wise, sir.

**FINCH.** And I will brazenly go there and *knock on her door.*

**MULLETT.** Very good, sir.

**FINCH.** And when I see her, I shall say: *"How is your dog?"* What do you think of that?

**MULLETT.** Love is a wonderful thing.

(**FINCH** *considers* **MULLETT** *for a moment.*)

**FINCH.** My pearl studs, Mullett – are they by any chance still in the drawer?

**MULLETT.** Safe and sound.

**FINCH.** I shall need them. Put me out a selection of ties – at least a dozen of them!

**MULLETT.** Yes, sir!

**FINCH.** Then go down to the Purple Chicken and *get some of it* –

**MULLETT.** I will *get a lot of it!*

**FINCH.** For we shall toast, Mullett. We shall toast to love!

## Sigsbee Waddington's Study. Evening.

(**SIGSBEE** *is in his chair. He wears a flannel shirt and a fringed vest. A set of chaps over his dress trousers. Red bandana 'round his neck. Cowboy boots. He is whittling with a Bowie knife.*)

(**FERRIS** *approaches him, carrying a set of evening clothes.*)

**SIGSBEE.** (*Expansive, joyous.*) Howdy-do, pardner!

**FERRIS.** (*British accent.*) I've brought your dinner clothing, Mr. Waddington.

**SIGSBEE.** Wheee Doggies!

**FERRIS.** Pardon me, sir?

**SIGSBEE.** Say "Wheee Doggies!", Ferris.

**FERRIS.** No thank you, sir.

**SIGSBEE.** Does the heart good, Ferris. Say: Wheee Doggies!

**FERRIS.** (*Flat.*) Wheee. Doggies.

**SIGSBEE.** There you go! HUP-HIP-HOODELEE-DOO! Now – bring me some moonshine, pardner. Somethin' strong and nasty – sure to make a lesser man hack up a lung.

**FERRIS.** Right away, sir. But, first, you must dress for dinner. The guests shall be arriving any moment.

**SIGSBEE.** The *effete elite of the East!*

**FERRIS.** Mrs. Waddington has insisted that you –

**SIGSBEE.** Those pinched and pampered little people – slaves to comfort, all of them! They wouldn't last a DAY out West! How 'bout you, Ferris: ever been OUT WEST?

**FERRIS.** I'm from England, sir. This *is* Out West.

**SIGSBEE.** *(Sings.\*)*
> OH GIVE ME A HOME
> WHERE THE BUFFALO ROAM

*(***MRS. WADDINGTON*** enters.)*

**MRS. WADDINGTON.** Is he pining for the West, again?

**FERRIS.** Oh, yes.

**SIGSBEE.**
> AND THE DEER AND THE ANTELOPE PLAY

**MRS. WADDINGTON.** Tonight of all nights!

**SIGSBEE.**
> WHERE SELDOM IS HEARD

**MRS. WADDINGTON.** Oh, Ferris, if my party is ruined –
imagine the gossip!

**SIGSBEE.**
> A DISCOURAGING WORD

**MRS. WADDINGTON.** I shall have to read about it in the
*Tattler.*

**FERRIS.** Indeed you would.

*(***FERRIS*** turns and goes, as –)*

*(***MRS. WADDINGTON*** approaches ***SIGSBEE.****)*

**SIGSBEE.**
> AND THE SKIES ARE NOT CLOUDY ALL –

---

\* A license to produce *Over the Moon* does not include a performance
license for any third-party or copyrighted music. Licensees should create
an original composition or use music in the public domain. For further
information, please see the Music and Third-Party Materials Use Note
on page iii.

**MRS. WADDINGTON.** SIGSBEE. *Do you know what tonight is?*

**SIGSBEE.** The vernal equinox?

*(He returns to his whittling.)*

**MRS. WADDINGTON.** It is the most important night of the year! The *creme de la creme* of greater New York – they're all arriving for dinner just now. And what's more, at my urging, Lord Pickering has travelled from London.

**SIGSBEE.** Why is HE here?

**MRS. WADDINGTON.** Why to dazzle our dear Molly, of course! In the end, it's all I want, Sigsbee: to see my daughter married to a fine young man of class and distinction.

**SIGSBEE.** She is your *step*-daughter.

**MRS. WADDINGTON.** Still: I have a reputation to maintain.

*(***FERRIS*** arrives with two drinks.)*

**FERRIS.** Cocktail, Madame?

**MRS. WADDINGTON.** No, thank you.

*(She grabs a glass and throws it down, in one gulp.)*

My *first husband* would never have pulled a *stunt* like this. No, sir: Mister P. Homer Horlick – the late, great Cheese King of Schenectady – he loved a good dinner party.

*(***SIGSBEE*** reaches for the second drink, but –)*

**SIGSBEE.** All Hail the Dead Cheese King.

*(– **MRS. WADDINGTON** grabs it and downs it, as well.)*

**MRS. WADDINGTON.** Ferris, I want all the Zane Grey books removed from this home!

**FERRIS.** With pleasure.

**SIGSBEE.** You'll never find 'em! I've got secrets, you know. I am one mysterious *hombre!*

**MRS. WADDINGTON.** That's it, Sigsbee: I've half a mind to *stop your allowance.*

> *(This gets his attention.)*

**SIGSBEE.** Why would you do *that?*

**MRS. WADDINGTON.** Any pocket money I give you goes to *chaps* and *spurs* and books about *smoking your own meat.*

**SIGSBEE.** Because I'm a MAN OF THE WEST.

**MRS. WADDINGTON.** Sigsbee Waddington, you've never been further west than *East Orange, New Jersey.*

**SIGSBEE.** But someday, when I'm calling the shots – when we're not living off your money from the Dead Cheese King – SOMEDAY I'll pack you up and take you out West!

**MRS. WADDINGTON.** That day, Sigsbee, will *never ever come.* Now: Get. Dressed.

> **(SIGSBEE** *stares at her, then grabs the clothes from* **FERRIS** *and starts out, just as –)*

> **(MOLLY** *enters.)*

**MOLLY.** Mother, everyone's waiting for you.

**SIGSBEE.** *(As he goes, defeated.)* Howdy-do, Molly.

**MOLLY.** Papa – what's wrong?

> *(But* **SIGSBEE** *is gone.* **FERRIS** *follows him off.)*

**MRS. WADDINGTON.** *(All smiles.)* So, tell me, Molly...have you seen Lord Pickering?

**MOLLY.** Yes, I have.

**MRS. WADDINGTON.** So handsome.

**MOLLY.** Yes.

**MRS. WADDINGTON.** Such breeding.

**MOLLY.** It would seem.

**MRS. WADDINGTON.** And his clothing –

**MOLLY.** Beyond belief.

**MRS. WADDINGTON.** Oh, I know – isn't he *dreamy!* I should be very happy, Molly, to see you married to a man like Lord Pickering.

**MOLLY.** Yes, I know. But I sometimes wonder if manners and breeding and wealth are the only things a woman should look for in a man.

**MRS. WADDINGTON.** Well –

**MOLLY.** I wonder if there isn't something to be said for the shy fellow with kind eyes who hides across the street for days on end.

**MRS. WADDINGTON.** What are you talking about?

**MOLLY.** The man who tries to speak to you – but instead, he sort of *chokes and turns pink and twists his fingers and makes funny noises through his nose* –

**MRS. WADDINGTON.** Molly! WHO IS THIS CHOKING-TWISTING-NOISE-THROUGH-THE-NOSE-MAN?!

**MOLLY.** I don't know, Mother. I haven't met him.

(**MRS. WADDINGTON** *starts off.*)

*(A wry smile.)* Not, yet.

## The Sidewalk Outside the Waddington Home.

(**FINCH** *is pacing. Adjusting his tie again and again. Unconvinced, he quickly pulls numerous alternate ties from his pocket and considers them – holding them against his chest in a panic of indecision. As he is doing this –)*

(**SIGSBEE** *appears. He has dutifully changed into his dinner clothes – but still sports his cowboy hat. He sees* **FINCH**.)

**SIGSBEE**.  Take it downtown, fella!

(**FINCH** *jumps, turns.)*

The last thing this city needs is another *itinerant haberdasher.*

(**FINCH** *is attempting to hide the ties with mixed success.)*

**FINCH**.  I assure you – it's not what you think.

**SIGSBEE**.  Oh, so you *know what I THINK, DO YOU?!*

**FINCH**.  No, I didn't mean to imply –

**SIGSBEE**.  FERRIS, REMOVE THIS MAN AT ONCE.

(**FERRIS** *appears and begins to usher* **FINCH** *away.)*

**FERRIS**.  Yes, sir.

**FINCH**.  Is this the home of Sigsbee H. Waddington?

**SIGSBEE**.  So what if it is?

**FINCH**.  Are *you* Mister Waddington?

**SIGSBEE**.  So what if I am?

**FERRIS.** That's enough now, let's –

**FINCH.** *(Desperate.)* I'm from Idaho, sir. And ever since I moved to New York, I have –

**SIGSBEE.** WHOA.

(**FERRIS** *stops.*)

*What did you say?*

**FINCH.** Ever since I –

**SIGSBEE.** *(Quickly.)* Before that.

**FINCH.** Are you Mister –

**SIGSBEE.** *(Quickly.)* After that.

**FINCH.** *I'm from Idaho?*

**SIGSBEE.** The West! Oh, my blessed stars: this man is *from the West!* FERRIS, UNHAND THIS FINE COWBOY.

**FERRIS.** But, sir –

**SIGSBEE.** How dare you treat a man from God's own country like he's some soul-bereft Eastern nose-bag?!

(**FERRIS** *lets go of* **FINCH.**)

They wouldn't stand for that in Idaho! They'd brand yer butt like a runaway steer! Ferris: set our new cowpoke a place at dinner.

**FERRIS.** *(Flat.)* Dinner, sir?

**SIGSBEE.** As my guest!

(**FERRIS** *goes.*)

**FINCH.** Mr. Waddington, that's quite nice of –

**SIGSBEE.** *Right good.*

**FINCH.** That's *right good* of you, sir – but are you sure Mrs. Waddington won't object?

**SIGSBEE.**  Do I look like the kind of man who gets bossed around by his wife?!

(**FERRIS** *reappears, quickly.*)

**FERRIS.**  Mister Waddington: your wife says you must come at once or have your allowance revoked.

(**SIGSBEE** *urgently waves* **FERRIS** *away.*)

**SIGSBEE.**  Say, listen – what's your name?

**FINCH.**  Finch. George Finch

**SIGSBEE.**  You married, Winch?

**FINCH.**  Finch.

**SIGSBEE.**  How do you mean "finch"?

**FINCH.**  You called me Winch.

**SIGSBEE.**  Why would I do that?

**FINCH.**  I think you thought it was my name.

(*As he talks,* **SIGSBEE** *removes a fountain pen from his coat and shoves it into his mouth – certain that it's a cigar.*)

**SIGSBEE.**  If your name is Winch, just say so! Let your Yea be your Yea, and your Nay be your Nay.

**FINCH.**  Yea, sir.

**SIGSBEE.**  You married, Pinch?

**FINCH.**  As a matter of fact: I'm not.

**SIGSBEE.**  I never said you were.

**FINCH.**  But you asked me if I was.

**SIGSBEE.**  And your reply was?

**FINCH.**  Nay, I'm not.

**SIGSBEE**. I don't like this beating around the bush, Pinch! It's not Western of you.

**FINCH**. I'm sorry, sir.

**SIGSBEE**. The Secret – and I say this as an older and wiser and better-looking man – the Secret to a successful marriage is this:

> (**SIGSBEE** *takes a long, thoughtful drag on his "cigar".*)

*Financial Independence.* When you marry, make sure you have *money of your own.* When I married my first wife – the mother of my dear Molly – back then, I was a wealthy man. Generous to a fault. I bought Molly's mother a pearl necklace that cost fifty-thousand dollars. Cash.

**FINCH**. That must be quite a necklace.

> (*Offering* **FINCH** *another fountain pen, still unaware.*)

**SIGSBEE**. Cigar.

**FINCH**. No, thank you.

**SIGSBEE**. But shortly after I married again, I lost all my money through bad investments – and I became completely dependent on my second wife. Pinch: you're looking at a man who is no longer master in his own home.

> (**SIGSBEE** *now looks at his "cigar".*)

This damn cigar won't draw.

**FINCH**. I think it's a fountain pen.

**SIGSBEE**. Isn't that typical of the East! You ask for cigars and they sell you fountain pens!

**FINCH**. Mister Waddington, if I may –

**SIGSBEE.**  You know what my wife's latest scheme is? To marry off my dear Molly to some haircut in spats named Lord Pickering.

**FINCH.**  *(Devastated.)* So – Molly is to be married?!

**SIGSBEE.**  Don't worry – I'll see that you're invited to the wedding.

**FINCH.**  But, is there nothing I can do?

**SIGSBEE.**  You can make a plan. Every man needs a plan.

**FINCH.**  Such as?

**SIGSBEE.**  There's a company in California – that's the *West*, you know – and this company is in the business of making *motion pictures*. And their motion pictures are said to be finer and better than any others being made.

That's why they're called the Finer and Better Motion Picture Company of California. And that's why I pulled a fast one and *bought one hundred shares of their stock!* How's THAT for a plan?!

> *(**MOLLY** appears, with some urgency.)*

**MOLLY.**  Papa, you really must –

> *(And now **MOLLY** sees **FINCH**. They lock eyes, frozen in place.)*

**SIGSBEE.**  Molly, I want you to meet a great buddy of mine from the West: this is Mister Clinch.

**FINCH.**  Actually, it's Finch.

**SIGSBEE.**  Finch-Pinch-Puddin'-an'-Pie! What's it matter what a man is called, as long as he talks straight and rides hard.

**MOLLY.**  Oh, it matters, Papa. It matters to a woman.

> *(To **FINCH**.)*

Hello.

**FINCH.** Umm...hello.

> *(Silence, as* **MOLLY** *and* **FINCH** *stare at one another.)*

**SIGSBEE.** What's wrong, Pinch – cat got yer giddyup? Go ahead: *say something.*

> *(More silence. Finally...)*

**FINCH.** *(Blurts out.) How is your dog?*

**MOLLY.** My *dog?*

**FINCH.** Yes – I feared that with all the excitement – the traffic and danger and confusion – I feared that a kind of *canine dementia* may have befallen him – that he may have gone all higgledy-piggledy in the head and had a sort of DOGGIE BREAKDOWN!

**MOLLY.** *(Strong.)* I must tell you, that is the most...

> *(Her voice softens.)*

...*endearing* thing I've ever heard. Did you hear that, Papa?

> *(***SIGSBEE** *plops his cowboy hat onto* **FINCH**'s *head, saying –)*

**SIGSBEE.** See you inside, cowpoke!

> *(***SIGSBEE** *goes.)*

> *(***FINCH** *and* **MOLLY** *stand there.)*

**MOLLY.** So, you're from out West?

**FINCH.** East Gilead.

**MOLLY.** Pardon?

**FINCH.** A little town in Idaho.

**MOLLY.** Must be nice out there.

**FINCH.** Very nice.

**MOLLY.** Prairies and mountains and all that sort of thing.

**FINCH.** Everywhere you look.

**MOLLY.** And you're a cowboy?

**FINCH.** What? Oh – no.

(*He takes off the cowboy hat.*)

Actually... I'm an artist. I paint pictures.

**MOLLY.** *Really?*

**FINCH.** I have a studio in Sheridan Square.

**MOLLY.** You must know Mister Beamish.

**FINCH.** Indeed, I do.

**MOLLY.** Mister Beamish has told me about a place called the Purple Chicken.

(*Whispers.*)

He says you can *get it* there.

**FINCH.** Oh, yes. If they know you, you can most definitely *get it.*

**MOLLY.** You're sure?

**FINCH.** Oh, yes. You can *go there,* and, well, just *get as much of it as you* want.

**MOLLY.** If they *know you.*

**FINCH.** And they *know ME!* Oh, boy, do they ever. I can get it *all the time*!

**MOLLY.** I'd like to go there.

**FINCH.** Oh, me too.

**MOLLY.** And I'd like to *get it.*

**FINCH.** Oh, *me too.*

**MOLLY**. And you know what else I'd like?

**FINCH**. *Please tell me.*

**MOLLY**. I'd like to see your paintings.

**FINCH**. You're kidding?!

**MOLLY**. Oh, if you don't show them, I understand.

**FINCH**. No one's ever asked to see them! I'll bring you as many as you'd like – by the *armload* – by the *crateful* –

> (**MRS. WADDINGTON** *appears.* **FERRIS** *is behind her.*)

**MRS. WADDINGTON**. Molly, dear – Lord Pickering is looking everywhere for you.

**MOLLY**. I was talking to Mister Finch. He is an artist.

**MRS. WADDINGTON**. How *interesting.*

**MOLLY**. He's offered to show me his work.

**MRS. WADDINGTON**. What a *surprise.*

**MOLLY**. And what's more, he's from out West. Papa has invited him to join us for dinner.

**MRS. WADDINGTON**. Well, doesn't that just *top it off with a cherry.* Why don't you go in and join the party. I'll be glad to escort Mister Finch.

**MOLLY**. *(To* **FINCH**.*)* I'll see you inside.

> (**MOLLY** *goes.*)

> (**MRS. WADDINGTON** *gives* **FINCH** *a head-to-toe stare.*)

**MRS. WADDINGTON**. So... I suppose you just *rode in from the hills?*

> (**FINCH** *immediately puts the cowboy hat behind his back.*)

**FINCH.** Oh, no, I –

**MRS. WADDINGTON.** Or perhaps you came here to *choke* and *turn pink?*

**FINCH.** *(As he does just that.)* Uh, certainly not, no –

**MRS. WADDINGTON.** To *twist your fingers* –

**FINCH.** In fact, no, I –

**MRS. WADDINGTON.** And to *make little noises through your nose?*

**FINCH.** Please, really, I can explain –

**MRS. WADDINGTON.** Ferris, how many are we at the table?

**FERRIS.** Twelve, Madame.

**MRS. WADDINGTON.** *(To* **FINCH.***)* It would be terribly bad luck to seat number thirteen. I'm sure you understand, *pardner.*

**FINCH.** *(Crushed.)* Oh. Yes. Of course.

**MRS. WADDINGTON.** *(A whisper to* **FERRIS.***)* Ferris, make certain that man is *never seen here again.*

**FERRIS.** With pleasure, Madame.

> *(***MRS. WADDINGTON** *is gone, as lights shift immediately to –)*

## The Roof. Day.

> *(***BEAMISH** *is doing exercises with two small barbells.)*

**BEAMISH.** Mullett tells me you've been goggling some woman up on the East Side.

**FINCH.** Oh, I've done more than goggle. I've learned her name! I had to go through the entire telephone directory to find out who lived at Sixteen East Seventy-Ninth Street. I started with the letter "A" –

**BEAMISH.** That is the home of the Waddingtons.

**FINCH.** – and *that's* why it took me all *week*.

**BEAMISH.** I'm a great friend of the family. And the woman you've been goggling must be their dear Molly.

**FINCH.** Yes – she tells me you've met.

**BEAMISH.** A wonderful young woman.

**FINCH.** I suppose you've been in her home?

**BEAMISH.** Of course.

**FINCH.** And dined with her?

**BEAMISH.** Certainly.

**FINCH.** *(Jealousy growing.)* And danced with her in your arms?

**BEAMISH.** In fact, I have.

**FINCH.** And when you looked in her eyes, you wanted to scale the skies and pluck out the stars and place them at her feet?!

**BEAMISH.** Impossible.

**FINCH.** Why?

**BEAMISH.** When you consider that the nearest star is *millions upon millions of* –

**FINCH.** You mean you're not in love with her?!

**BEAMISH.** Of course not.

**FINCH.** *(Incredulous.)* How can that be?! What's wrong with you?

　　　*(**MULLETT**, working, passes by.)*

**BEAMISH.** Mullett, I need that booklet.

(**MULLETT** *immediately fans out the many booklets* **BEAMISH** *gave him.*)

**MULLETT.** Which one, sir?

**BEAMISH.** "The Principles of Rational Matrimony."

(**BEAMISH** *takes the appropriate booklet, and hands it to* **FINCH.**)

In matters of love, George, the Mind Must Guide The Heart.

**FINCH.** Just you *wait*, Beamish. Wait till it happens to *you*.

**BEAMISH.** When I marry, George, it will be the result of a careful and deliberate three-stop process. *One*: I shall decide upon the best age for me to marry. *Two*: I shall compile a list of female friends and select one whose tastes are in harmony with my own. And, *Three:* when I am certain that passion has not blinded me to her faults, then, and only then, will I ask her to be wife.

**FINCH.** It sounds like you're picking out a *pair of shoes*.

**BEAMISH.** If people picked their spouses with the care they picked their shoes, we'd all see a better day. Now: when it comes to the Waddingtons, you would do well to observe a few hard and fast rules. *One*: never show up on their doorstep unannounced. *Two*: never mention that you are from "the West". And, *Three*: never EVER let on that you're an artist.

(*Off* **FINCH**'*s look.*)

You've done all of those, haven't you?

**FINCH.** Yes! – but Molly still asked to see my paintings!

**BEAMISH.** Surely that can be avoided.

**FINCH.** (*Proudly.*) I am an artist, Hamilton, and I don't care who knows it.

**BEAMISH.** I shouldn't worry, George, about anyone finding out. Listen now: there is nothing Mrs. Waddington *despises more than an artist* – those "pitiful paragons of poverty!"

**FINCH.** But I have plenty of money.

**BEAMISH.** From your inheritance, I know –

**FINCH.** Yes! I have LOADS of money. I'm RICH.

**BEAMISH.** – but how was she to know that?! You appear on her doorstep like a tumbleweed and naturally she assumes the worst.

**FINCH.** So, what can I *do?*

**BEAMISH.** I will speak to Molly myself. I'll convey to her, as *rationally* as possible, your genuine and abiding interest. And I will ascertain whether her pending affections are mutually directed.

**FINCH.** Okay, sure – but then tell her I think she HUNG THE MOON!

> (**FINCH** *shoves* **BEAMISH** *on his way toward* –)

## The Sidewalk Outside the Waddington Home. Day.

> (– *Just as* **MOLLY** *emerges from the door, wearing sunglasses, and intercepts him.*)

**MOLLY.** Oh, Mister Beamish – I'm so glad to see you. Mother has forbidden George to even enter the house. Simply because he doesn't have money.

**BEAMISH.** Well, in fact, that's something I wanted to talk to you about –

**MOLLY**.  I'm GLAD he has no money! Among his many virtues is the fact George Finch is NOT RICH.

**BEAMISH**.  Actually, Molly –

**MOLLY**.  And what's more: we don't need his money. When we are married, I shall inherit the *pearl necklace* that Papa bought my mother years ago. I will sell that necklace for *thousands of dollars* – and George will be able to paint as many pictures as he likes!

**BEAMISH**.  Heaven help us all.

**MOLLY**.  Here's my plan: Mother goes to see her fortune teller once a week. Whatever appears in the crystal ball, Mother believes without reservation.

**BEAMISH**.  A crystal ball is nothing but *hocus-pocus* – completely irrational!

**MOLLY**.  And that's where you come in. You will go to the fortune teller and offer a bribe. Ask her to foresee nothing but trouble in a marriage to Lord Pickering. And ask her to mention the initials: "G. F." Will you do that?

**BEAMISH**.  Of course I will. George Finch is a capital fellow. But, as for his finances –

**MOLLY**.  He's the *bee's knees*, is what he is. Make sure to tell him that – that he's the *bee's knees!*

(**MOLLY** *quickly goes back inside, just as –*)

(**FINCH** *appears at* **BEAMISH**'s *side.*)

**FINCH**.  Well?! Did you tell her I think she *hung the moon?*

**BEAMISH**.  Not in so many words, but –

**FINCH**.  What then?! What did she say about me?!

**BEAMISH**.  She referred to you...

**FINCH**.  Yes?

**BEAMISH**. As the *central joint in the leg of a honey-making insect.*

**FINCH**. Oh, I am stung!

**BEAMISH**. And I am late. Goodbye, Romeo.

> (**BEAMISH** *gives* **FINCH** *a shove, as he turns and approaches –*)

## Madame Eulalie's Salon.

> (*A woman sits, with beautiful scarf (or veil) covering her head and face. In front of her is a small table which holds a crystal ball.*)

**BEAMISH**. Good afternoon. Miss Molly Waddington sent me.

> (*"you-LAY-lee".*)

I'm looking for a "Madame Eulalie". I'm told she is a fortune teller.

**MADAME EULALIE**. (*A mysterious voice.*) I see nothing.

**BEAMISH**. Oh, very well.

**MADAME EULALIE**. Nothing at all.

**BEAMISH**. I understand.

**MADAME EULALIE**. Can you help me?

**BEAMISH**. Sorry?

**MADAME EULALIE**. I have something in my eye.

> (*Drops mysterious voice.*)

A speck of dust, I think.

**BEAMISH**. Well, then: permit me.

> (*He moves close to her. As he speaks, he lifts the scarf...*)

Few people are aware what a difficult task it is. When an ordinary man is faced with a foreign body in the eye of a...

> (*... And he sees her face. It stops him in his tracks.*)

**BEAMISH**. ...simply *perfect stranger* of the opposite...*sex*... well, there is just...*no booklet* to prepare you for *that*.

> (*His work is done. She dabs at her eyes with his handkerchief. They are still face to face.*)

**MADAME EULALIE**. Thank you so much.

> (**BEAMISH***'s mouth is open, as though he's trying to speak – but nothing whatsoever is coming out.*)

Why is it, do you suppose, that something so small can have such a momentous effect?

> (*He stares. Dumbfounded. In love.*)

**BEAMISH**. Ummmmmmmm...

**MADAME EULALIE**. You said you were sent to find me?

**BEAMISH**. By the hand of Fate.

**MADAME EULALIE**. Shall I read your palm?

> (*He instantly extends his hand. She traces its lines with her fingers.*)

You have a strong, dominating nature; iron determination; great breadth of vision; a keen, incisive mind. And yet, with it all, you are gentle at heart, kind and loyal, generous to a fault. Shall I continue?

**BEAMISH**. Don't ever stop.

(**GARROWAY** *appears. He wears the clothes of a "dandy" – lavender gloves, a white scarf, as well as the beret he wore earlier.*)

**GARROWAY.** Mister Delancy Cabot to see you, ma'am.

| **MADAME EULALIE.** | **BEAMISH.** |
|---|---|
| Who? | What? |

**GARROWAY.** Cabot. Delancy Cabot. I have a one-o'clock appointment.

(**BEAMISH** *turns and sees him.*)

**BEAMISH.** Garroway! What the devil are you doing here?

**GARROWAY.** Mister Beamish!

**BEAMISH.** Why are you calling yourself –

**GARROWAY.** Delancy Cabot. I thought it might be my *nom de plume.*

**BEAMISH.** And what are you *wearing?*! Since when does a policeman wear the clothes of a *bell hop at a fun-house?!*

**GARROWAY.** This is my *undercover disguise!*

**MADAME EULALIE.** *(Worried.)* Did you say: *policeman?*

**BEAMISH.** Indeed I did.

(*In an instant,* **MADAME EULALIE** *has covered the crystal ball with a cloth, produced a nail file and other implements – and is giving* **BEAMISH** *a manicure.*)

**MADAME EULALIE.** *(To* **GARROWAY.***)* Welcome to the salon. I'll be right with you.

| **GARROWAY.** | **BEAMISH.** |
|---|---|
| *Salon?* | *Salon?* |

**MADAME EULALIE.**  Hold still, mister. Your manicure's nearly done.

(**BEAMISH** *instantly plays along.*)

**BEAMISH.**  Garroway: this is a *bad time.* Do you understand?

**GARROWAY.**  I didn't know Madame Eulalie was a friend of yours.

**BEAMISH.**  Indeed she is. I often come here to have my palm –

(*Catches her eye.*)

*Rubbed.* My fingers – *filed.* Nothing tops good grooming, Garroway.

**GARROWAY.**  Yes, sir – but we got a tip that this woman was *telling fortunes in exchange for payment.* I was sent here to give her the pinch!

**BEAMISH.**  Garroway – how dare you try to nail a manicurist when you should be off polishing your poem.

**GARROWAY.**  I finished it, sir. Want to hear it?

**BEAMISH.**  *Now?*

**GARROWAY.**  I have it right here in my notebook.

(**GARROWAY** *removes his notebook from a pocket. Opens it. Clears his throat. And reads.*)

"Streets!"

**BEAMISH.**  That is the title?

**GARROWAY.**  Yes, sir. And also the first line.

**BEAMISH.**  So I feared.

**GARROWAY.**  *(With great passion.)* Streets!
Stark, grim, perilous streets!

Crying, dying, stultifying streets!

I pace and pace,

Dogs snap and growl,

And from my throat

A feral howl:

Loathsome, leering, lecherous streets!

Rancid, rabid, rancorous streets!

Putrid, fetid, festering stre –

**BEAMISH.** *(Aghast.)* STOP. Garroway, your poem is WRONG-WRONG-WRONG. Wrong in every conceivable way.

(**GARROWAY** *lowers the notebook.*)

**GARROWAY.** But you said to be stark and grim.

**BEAMISH.** Nothing of the sort.

(*Looking at* **MADAME EULALIE**.)

A poem, Garroway, should be about one thing, and one thing only: *love.*

**GARROWAY.** But –

**BEAMISH.** Only love can inspire the bard within.

**GARROWAY.** But –

**BEAMISH.** Go, Garroway! Go and walk those streets with a little skip in your step, and your eyes on the lookout for love!

(**GARROWAY** *dutifully skips away.*)

**MADAME EULALIE.** Did he say Beamish?

**BEAMISH.** *(Extends hand.)* Hamilton J. At your service.

**MADAME EULALIE.** Not THE Hamilton J. Beamish? Of the BOOKLETS?

**BEAMISH.** Well, yes, I've written a few booklets in my day.

**MADAME EULALIE**. You're my favorite author. If it hadn't been for you, I'd still be moldering in a little one-horse town out West. But once I read "Find Yourself a Groove and Get In It!" – I packed up, moved to New York, and never looked back.

**BEAMISH**. The "Get in Your Groove" series has been quite popular.

**MADAME EULALIE**. Oh, if I'd known you were Hamilton J. Beamish when you walked in, I might have embarrassed myself.

**BEAMISH**. I could come in again.

**MADAME EULALIE**. *(Smiles.)* Why would Miss Waddington send you to me?

**BEAMISH**. Molly's mother is determined to marry her off to a Lord Pickering – a fate Molly wishes to avoid at all costs. Therefore she hoped you could, in your next session, contrive a rather dark premonition regarding this marriage. To – well – sort of –

**MADAME EULALIE**. Scare the bejesus out of the old bag.

**BEAMISH**. Precisely!

**MADAME EULALIE**. Because Molly must be in love with another man.

**BEAMISH**. His initials are "G. F." And he's madly in love with her.

**MADAME EULALIE**. And you're not?

**BEAMISH**. Oh, no. I am in love with –

*(Stops, staring at her.)*

A...little...Purple...Chicken.

**MADAME EULALIE**. How very odd.

**BEAMISH**. It's a *cafe*. A place where, if you play your cards right, you can *get it*.

**MADAME EULALIE.** I see.

**BEAMISH.** Would you like to *get it* someday?

**MADAME EULALIE.** When?

**BEAMISH.** Tomorrow?

**MADAME EULALIE.** I'm afraid I'm leaving town.

**BEAMISH.** The day after?

**MADAME EULALIE.** I'll be gone three weeks. Back home for Pop's birthday.

**BEAMISH.** But when you return?

**MADAME EULALIE.** Oh, I'd love to *get it* with you then.

**BEAMISH.** Oh, thank you, Madame Eu –

**MADAME EULALIE.** *("LAY-lee".)* Lalie.

**BEAMISH.** "Lalie." Like a flower in a meadow.

**MADAME EULALIE.** Till then, Mister Bea –

**BEAMISH.** Hamilton.

**MADAME EULALIE.** No. Too stiff. What's your middle name?

**BEAMISH.** Well, that would be "James".

**MADAME EULALIE.** I'll call you *Jimmy*. Isn't that better?

**BEAMISH.** *Oh, yes.*

**MADAME EULALIE.** Till then, Jimmy.

> (**MADAME EULALIE** *is gone.* **BEAMISH** *ends up holding her scarf – which he drapes around his neck as he turns and arrives at –)*

### The Roof. Day.

**FINCH.** *Jimmy?* She calls you *Jimmy?*

**BEAMISH.** Only *she* can say it the way it's *meant to be said.*

**FINCH.** Beamish: you're in love!

**BEAMISH.** So what if I am?

**FINCH.** With a woman you've seen only ONCE!

**BEAMISH.** So, what if I have?

**FINCH.** What happened to "The Mind must guide the Heart"?

**BEAMISH.** Well – as you know – one *develops.* One *evolves.*

**FINCH.** What does she look like?

**BEAMISH.** She has eyes like the mists of sunrise floating over some magic pool in Fairyland.

**FINCH.** *(Smiles.)* Welcome to the club.

**BEAMISH.** *(As he holds* **FINCH.***)* Oh, I just want to seize her and hold her close and kiss her and kiss her again and again and again and again!

**FINCH.** All right, then: get a hold of yourself *and let go of me* and tell me everything that Molly said.

**BEAMISH.** You're to meet her at the zoo tomorrow. She'll look for you near the lions.

**FINCH.** And she will hear me roar!

**BEAMISH.** *(A cry to the heavens.)* Oh, what a thing is love!

**FINCH.** C'mon, friend –

**BEAMISH.** But how will I wait three weeks to see her again?!

**FINCH.** Let's go *get a little*!

> (**FINCH** *and* **BEAMISH** *rush off, as lights return to –)*

## Madame Eulalie's Salon.

(**MRS. WADDINGTON** *sits across from* **MADAME EULALIE** – *who is peering into her crystal ball.*)

**MADAME EULALIE.** The mists begin to clear away...and the mysteries appear...

**MRS. WADDINGTON.** You're seeing something already?

**MADAME EULALIE.** A young woman...a relative of yours... I see the letter "M"...

**MRS. WADDINGTON.** That's Molly – my stepdaughter!

**MADAME EULALIE.** She wears a wedding dress...she is walking down an aisle –

**MRS. WADDINGTON.** Oh, goody. Keep going –

**MADAME EULALIE.** She is on the arm of a man – British, perhaps – I see the letter...

**MRS. WADDINGTON.** "P"? The letter "P"? For Lord Pickering?!

**MADAME EULALIE.** I see the letter "P."

**MRS. WADDINGTON.** I knew it! Oh, he's an exceptional man – the sole heir to a large endowment set up by his father.

**MADAME EULALIE.** Yes – I see this well-endowed young man walking your stepdaughter down the aisle –

**MRS. WADDINGTON.** Oh, blessed day!

**MADAME EULALIE.** But now, suddenly, there is a commotion –

**MRS. WADDINGTON.** What?

**MADAME EULALIE.** – and from the crowd a woman stands up – a Woman in Black – a Wronged Woman – she is distraught – screaming at the groom – claiming he has injured her, broken her heart, ruined her life – and the groom gives her a villainous look –

**MRS. WADDINGTON.** Lord Pickering?

**MADAME EULALIE.** – he shoves her away with great force –

**MRS. WADDINGTON.** No!

**MADAME EULALIE.** – and she falls onto a table where all the wedding gifts are arrayed –

**MRS. WADDINGTON.** It can't be!

**MADAME EULALIE.** – and when she turns, *she is holding a revolver!*

**MRS. WADDINGTON.** No, please stop her!

**MADAME EULALIE.** She aims it at Lord Pickering – *but Molly has rushed to his side – leapt in front to protect him* – JUST AS THE WRONGED WOMAN PULLS THE TRIGGER AND ...

**MRS. WADDINGTON.** Yes?! Yes?!

(**MADAME EULALIE** *leans back.*)

**MADAME EULALIE.** The vision fades.

**MRS. WADDINGTON.** There must be some mistake!

**MADAME EULALIE.** The crystal never deceives.

**MRS. WADDINGTON.** But, my dear Molly – what will I do with her?

**MADAME EULALIE.** *(Looks into the crystal.)* Wait.

**MRS. WADDINGTON.** What?

**MADAME EULALIE.** Two lingering letters...a "G" ...and an "F."

**MRS. WADDINGTON.** "G. F."?

**MADAME EULALIE.**  And around these letters: an aura of warmth. A fine, contented glow.

>   (**MRS. WADDINGTON** *is staring into the crystal in disbelief.*)

**MRS. WADDINGTON.**  "G. F."? – have you nothing more to tell me?!

**MADAME EULALIE.**  That will be ten dollars, please.


## Sigsbee Waddington's Study. Afternoon.

>   (**MOLLY** *and* **SIGSBEE** *are there, as* **MRS. WADDINGTON** *arrives.*)

**SIGSBEE.**  Ah, there you are. Dear.

**MRS. WADDINGTON.**  Ferris said the two of you wanted to see me.

**SIGSBEE.**  Yes. Dear.

**MRS. WADDINGTON.**  Whenever you call me "dear" you're always about to tell me something terrible.

**SIGSBEE.**  *(Very nervous.)* Well...do you remember that splendid young Westerner named Quinch –

**MOLLY.**  *(Quick whisper.)* Finch.

**SIGSBEE.**  – who was kind enough to stop by a few nights ago?

**MRS. WADDINGTON.**  I made it known that he was never to return.

**SIGSBEE.**  Yes, well, I think that may change now. Dear.

**MRS. WADDINGTON.**  *(Leans in to him.)* Go on.

**SIGSBEE.**  Because – well – the fact is...

(**SIGSBEE** *freezes.* **MOLLY** *gives up on him and steps forward –*)

**MOLLY**.  The fact is: George has asked me to marry him!

**MRS. WADDINGTON**.  *What did you say?!*

**MOLLY**.  By the most extraordinary chance, George and I happened to meet at the zoo today. We talked for a good long while and one thing led to the next and before I knew it he had asked me to marry him outside the cage of the Siberian yak.

**SIGSBEE**.  Absolutely not! You'll be married at St. Patrick's like any other respectable girl.

**MRS. WADDINGTON**.  You will do NO SUCH THING. I will not allow you to ruin your life by marrying a despicable fortune-hunter.

**MOLLY**.  He is not a fortune-hunter!

(*Proudly.*)

George Finch is a penniless artist!

**MRS. WADDINGTON**.  Exactly! He could never support you!

**MOLLY**.  He doesn't need to! When I marry, I get the pearl necklace that Papa gave to Mama years ago. And when I sell that, we'll have plenty of money. Right, Papa?!

(*Hearing this,* **SIGSBEE** *immediately plops down in his chair, his head between his legs, moaning and stomping his feet, repeatedly.*)

**MRS. WADDINGTON**.  Sigsbee – what on earth is the matter?

**SIGSBEE**.  *Honey, I don't think it would be wise to sell that necklace!*

**MOLLY**.  Don't worry, Papa. I won't miss it.

SIGSBEE. *But, listen –*

MOLLY. I don't need jewelry. I'm in love!

> (**SIGSBEE** *instantly returns to his moaning and stomping, as –*)

> (**FERRIS** *appears.*)

FERRIS. Mister Beamish and Mister Finch.

> (**FERRIS** *goes.*)

> (**BEAMISH** *steps in, happily. He is attached to* **FINCH** *via handcuffs. Finch's suit is filthy and torn, missing one sleeve. One of his shoes is gone. His non-handcuffed arm is in a sling. He has a dirty face, a black eye and bandage on his head. He's a wreck.*)

BEAMISH. Here we are! How's everyone?

MRS. WADDINGTON. My daughter is not going to marry... THAT.

MOLLY. Dear George – what's happened to you?

FINCH. Oh, any number of things.

BEAMISH. Our lovesick George was so happy after Molly accepted his proposal that he began to hand out dollar bills on the corner of fifty-ninth and fifth –

MOLLY. See how generous he is? And with so little money to his name!

BEAMISH. – and soon thereafter, a bit of a *riot* ensued – and George was hauled off in the paddy wagon. I posted his bail and he was released into my custody.

MRS. WADDINGTON. Well, you can haul him right back to the police!

**BEAMISH.** Come now, Mrs. Waddington: what is your objection to my dear friend?

**MRS. WADDINGTON.** He is an *artist.*

**BEAMISH.** Still and all –

**MRS. WADDINGTON.** He belongs to that feckless breed of *bohemians* who wear strange costumes, attend dubious parties, and often play the ukulele!

**MOLLY.** He DOES NOT play the ukulele!

**BEAMISH.** The fact is: George happens to have the one quality that no great artist ever had.

**MRS. WADDINGTON.** And what is that?

**BEAMISH.** He cannot paint.

| **FINCH.** | **MOLLY.** |
|---|---|
| Beamish! | That's not true! |

**BEAMISH.** Not a *whit.* Not to *save his life!* He is perhaps *the worst artist in the history of New York City!*

**MRS. WADDINGTON.** And thus he cannot expect to make a penny off his work!

**BEAMISH.** Is that your chief objection? That George has no money?

**FINCH.** The fact is, Mrs. Waddington, I have –

**BEAMISH.** I'll handle this, George.

        *(To* **MRS. WADDINGTON.***)*

Are you saying you would give your consent to this marriage if you discovered that George Finch was a wealthy man?

**MRS. WADDINGTON.** I would *consider it.*

**BEAMISH.** Well, then, let me tell you this: George Finch just happens to be an exceedingly –

**MOLLY.** Sweet and tender and generous man! I'm going to marry him THREE WEEKS FROM TODAY! And I'm going to sell that pearl necklace FIRST CHANCE I GET.

(**SIGSBEE** *returns to moaning and stomping again, as –*)

(**FINCH** *turns to* **MRS. WADDINGTON.**)

**FINCH.** *(With great kindness.)* Mother.

**MRS. WADDINGTON.** *(Ice.) What did you call me?*

(**FINCH** *moves toward* **MRS. WADDINGTON** – *dragging* **BEAMISH** *along with him.*)

**FINCH.** I called you "Mother." I want you to know the affection with which I regard you.

**MOLLY.** Isn't that sweet?

(**MRS. WADDINGTON** *is now close enough to* **FINCH** *to read the monogram on his tie. She freezes.*)

**MRS. WADDINGTON.** The monogram on your tie. "G. F."

(*She lifts her head and looks* **FINCH** *in the eye, horrified.*)

**FINCH.** You can call me "son."

**MRS. WADDINGTON.** FERRIS, I NEED A DRINK.

(**MRS. WADDINGTON** *rushes out.*)

**MOLLY.** Promise me, George: that you'll never, ever be a wealthy man.

**FINCH.** *(Off a nod from* **BEAMISH.**) I promise.

**SIGSBEE.** Beamish, I need to speak to you! In private!

**BEAMISH.** *(Re: handcuffs.)* I'm afraid that's not possible.

(**FERRIS** *arrives with a large drink for* **MRS. WADDINGTON** – *who is gone.*)

**FERRIS.** *(Looking for her.)* Your drink – Mrs. Waddington?

**SIGSBEE.** It's urgent, Beamish!

(**SIGSBEE** *grabs the drink and downs it, as –*)

(**BEAMISH** *grabs* **FERRIS.**)

**BEAMISH.** Very well. Ferris: I *deputize you.*

(**BEAMISH** *quickly removes the handcuffs from his own wrist – and attaches* **FINCH** *to* **FERRIS.**)

Don't worry. He's no trouble at all.

**MOLLY.** C'mon – we've got loads of planning to do!

(**MOLLY** *takes* **FINCH** *by the arm and they exit, dragging* **FERRIS** *along with them.*)

**BEAMISH.** You must be very proud.

**SIGSBEE.** I'm cooked, is what I am! Molly will never forgive me!

*(From his pocket,* **SIGSBEE** *removes a small velvet box.)*

The pearls in this necklace are *fakes*. I sold the real ones and bought stock in a motion picture company –

(**SIGSBEE** *produces a stock certificate. Shows it to* **BEAMISH.**)

– always planning, of course, to restore the *real pearls* once my ship comes in.

**BEAMISH.** I'm afraid your ship has sunk.

**SIGSBEE.** What?!

**BEAMISH**. The "Finer and Better Motion Picture Company" went out of business last year. They never made a picture.

**SIGSBEE**. So, it's worthless?!

**BEAMISH**. Absolutely.

**SIGSBEE**. WHAT CAN I DO?

**BEAMISH**. Short of *stealing the necklace back* before Molly tries to sell it – there's nothing to be done. Goodbye, Mister Waddington.

    (**BEAMISH** *goes.*)

**SIGSBEE**. STEALING THE NECKLACE?! What kind of father would steal a necklace from his own daughter? Clearly a very...

    (*Complete change in tone.*)

...*brilliant father* – that's who! Hup-hip-hoodelee-doo!

    (**SIGSBEE** *rushes off.*)

## The Roof. Sunset.

    (**GARROWAY** *stands, peering out at the city. He holds his notebook. He is composing a poem. It is not going well.*)

**GARROWAY**. Love is – a *dove*. Love is – *above*. Love is – a *dove* that we *shove* with a *glove* from *above*.

    (**MULLETT** *crosses the roof towards* **FINCH***'s apartment. He carries a bag of groceries. He tries to avoid* **GARROWAY**.)

Evening, Mullett.

**MULLETT**. So it is.

*(A sound from the apartment: pots and pans falling to the ground.)*

**GARROWAY**. *(Re: the sound.)* Is Mister Finch in?

**MULLETT**. No – he's out.

**GARROWAY**. *(Suspicious.)* Then who's in there?

**MULLETT**. Oh, that's my bride-to-be.

**GARROWAY**. So you're in *love*, are you?

**MULLETT**. *(Turning to go.)* You bet I am. Have a good night.

**GARROWAY**. Maybe you can help me, Mullet. I'm trying to write about love, but all the good terms of endearment have already been used: "dear", "darling", "beloved" –

**FANNY'S VOICE**. POOOOOOKEEEEE!

*(They each turn towards the voice.)*

**MULLETT**. Pookee is the cat.

**FANNY'S VOICE**. POOKEE? – WHO ARE YOU TALKING TO?

**MULLETT**. I gotta go.

*(**MULLETT** goes quickly, as –)*

*(**SIGSBEE** enters, opposite.)*

**SIGSBEE**. Beamish? – are you up here?

*(Checks his pocket watch.)*

*It's nearly six-o'clock – where can you be?!*

**GARROWAY**. Mister Beamish lives two floors down – though he does conduct his poetry classes on this roof.

**SIGSBEE**. Poetry-*Schmoetry* – I need a thief! I paged through the telephone directory till my hands were blue - but there's not a single listing for "THIEVES"! Why must they omit the most crucial professions?

**GARROWAY.** I might be able to help you.

**SIGSBEE.** What could a policeman possibly know about thieves?

**GARROWAY.** I know there's one in that apartment right now. His name's Mullet.

**SIGSBEE.** You don't say. Well...suppose – just for kicks and giggles – that a very wicked fella wanted this crook to do a horrible, nasty thing? Would this crook want to be *paid?*

**GARROWAY.** Oh, yes, sir.

**SIGSBEE.** *(Nervously.)* How much?

**GARROWAY.** I would think a few hundred dollars, at least.

(**SIGSBEE** *is digging through his pockets, as he speaks –)*

**SIGSBEE.** But, I don't – I mean – *this wicked fella* doesn't carry around that kind of money!

**GARROWAY.** Well, he *should.* Never trust a bank with your money. I carry my entire life savings – three hundred bucks – right here in my hat.

(**SIGSBEE** *turns, considers this. He produces the stock certificate.)*

**SIGSBEE.** I'm sorry: I didn't get your name.

**GARROWAY.** Garroway, sir.

**SIGSBEE.** Do you like movies, Larrabee? Movies are *huge*, pardner. Bigger than steel! Bigger than beef! And nobody makes finer and better movies than the Finer and Better Motion Picture Company of Hollywood, California! Heard of them?

**GARROWAY.** No, sir.

**SIGSBEE.** Of course you haven't! NO ONE HAS! And that's the beauty of it! They're not one of those worn-out old companies that everyone's sick and tired of. They're brand new!

**GARROWAY.** You don't say.

(**SIGSBEE** *hands him the certificate.*)

**SIGSBEE.** And you'd be in on the ground floor!

**GARROWAY.** Have I seen any of their pictures?

**SIGSBEE.** Of course you haven't. NO ONE HAS! They don't waste their money on high-priced stars and fancy-pants directors. They don't even have a studio!

**GARROWAY.** Then how do they make their movies?

**SIGSBEE.** *I have no idea!* NO ONE DOES! All I know is that, in the current market, that stock is worth *thousands and thousands of dollars* – but I could let you have it for a piddling...three hundred bucks.

**GARROWAY.** You'd do that for me?

**SIGSBEE.** I see a policeman on a roof and I think: *what can I do to help that man?*

**GARROWAY.** Sounds like the opportunity of a lifetime.

**SIGSBEE.** Of SEVERAL LIFETIMES – in fact, now I see I'd be a FOOL to part with these shares –

(**SIGSBEE** *grabs the stock certificate back from* **GARROWAY**.)

**GARROWAY.** But, I have the money right here!

**SIGSBEE.** Well, you better hurry, Gaberdeen –

(**GARROWAY** *quickly removes his hat and counts out the money.*)

**GARROWAY.** One hundred –

**SIGSBEE.** Before I come to my senses –

**GARROWAY.** Two hundred –

**SIGSBEE.** And change my mind –

**GARROWAY.** Three hundred.

**SIGSBEE.** *Sold.*

> (**SIGSBEE** *gives him the certificate.*)

Now, run along and get filthy rich!

**GARROWAY.** Yes, sir!

> (*And* **GARROWAY** *rushes off into the stairwell, just as –*)

> (**FANNY** *emerges from* **FINCH**'s *apartment, happily calling back into the room –*)

**FANNY'S VOICE.** OH, POOKEE – YOU BAD, BAD BOY!

> (*As* **SIGSBEE** *turns toward the sound, he and* **FANNY** *bump headlong into each other.*)

**SIGSBEE.** Oh, I'm very sorry

**FANNY.** No problem, Pops!

> (*She starts towards the fire escape.*)

**SIGSBEE.** Excuse me – is Mister Gullett inside?

**FANNY.** *Mullett,* if you please. We've run out of champagne, so I'm off to *get a little.*

**SIGSBEE.** Say, listen: is it true that he dabbles in *the criminological arts?*

**FANNY.** You mean: is he a thief?

**SIGSBEE.** Yes.

**FANNY.** Not any more. A great waste of talent, if you ask me.

*(She starts off again.)*

**SIGSBEE.**  But I can pay him three hundred bucks!

*(She stops, at a distance.* **SIGSBEE** *has turned away.)*

**SIGSBEE.**  Slap-my-head-with-soda-bread: where am I going to find a thief at this hour?!

*(He is looking for his pocket watch.)*

That's odd. My pocket watch. I can't seem to –

*(And* **FANNY** *holds up the watch – letting it dangle from its chain.)*

**FANNY.**  Hi.

*(He looks up at her. Sees his watch.)*

I'm Fanny.

*(Lights out fast.)*

# ACT TWO

## The Roof. Morning.

(**MULLETT** *lifts and holds* **FANNY** *in his arms. They are newly married. She holds a bouquet of flowers. A small traveling bag is near them.*)

**FANNY.** It was the wedding I'd always dreamed of!

**MULLETT.** Nothin' but the best for the new Mrs. Mullett!

(*They each toss a handful of confetti into the air.*)

I'm sorry we had no reception – but I wanted to get back here as fast as we could.

**FANNY.** How long is Mister Finch gone?

**MULLETT.** Today and tomorrow. He's being married out on Long Island.

**FANNY.** Very inconvenient.

**MULLETT.** Mrs. Waddington demanded that the wedding be something *small and rural and very far away*. Good for us, though – we get his apartment all to ourselves! And right over there, Fanny – is a *sleeping porch.*

**FANNY.** Which I hope you don't plan to use for *sleeping.*

**MULLETT.** Oh, no I *don't.*

(*They kiss.*)

**MULLETT.**  And then, when our honeymoon's over, we'll go upstate and buy a little duck farm and live happily ever after.

**FANNY.**  *(Not keen on this.)* Oh, Freddy – can you really see me on a duck farm?

**MULLETT.**  Doesn't it sound perfect? After a life of crime – the chance to settle down with nothing but the quacking of the ducks, the droning of the bees, and the silver candlestick.

**FANNY.**  The...what?

>       (**MULLETT** *removes a silver candlestick from the traveling bag.*)

Now, how did *that* get there?

**MULLETT.**  We're retired now, Fanny. You promised.

**FANNY.**  But, wouldn't it be a crime to pass up something *big* – something that just *fell into our lap.*

>       (**FANNY** *takes the candlestick from* **MULLET.***)*

**MULLETT.**  The crime would be to get pinched and spend our honeymoon in the slammer.

**FANNY.**  Not to worry. If they ever nab me, I've got a yarn about me poor old Irish Mother that would draw tears from a stone: "DON'T TURN ME OVER TO THE BULLS, MISTER. I ONLY DID IT FOR ME DEAR OLD MA –"

**MULLETT.**  No one's going to nab you but *me*. Now: I've got *champagne waiting in the sleeping porch...*

>       (**MULLETT** *leads her to the sleeping porch door. He steps inside.*)

**FANNY.**  Sounds perfect. But, first I have to run a little errand.

**MULLETT.** *Today?*

**FANNY.** *(Kisses him quickly.)* Don't start without me!

> *(FANNY nudges MULLETT into the sleeping porch, as she heads toward the stairwell –)*

> *(– Where she bumps headlong into GARROWAY, who is just arriving.)*

**GARROWAY.** Oh, pardon me, miss.

**FANNY.** Don't mention it, Officer. Have a lovely day!

> *(FANNY is gone down the stairwell.)*

> *(GARROWAY turns and discovers that he has the silver candlestick in his hand. He stares at it, as –)*

> *(BEAMISH arrives from the stairwell. He is carrying a large daisy. He still wears the MADAME EULALIE scarf around his neck.)*

**BEAMISH.** Oh, look at this vista! And in every window of every home: happy, smiling people – dancing for joy.

> *(Turns to GARROWAY.)*

Well, go ahead, Garroway: read me something about *LOVE.*

> *(BEAMISH begins pulling the petals, one by one, off the daisy.)*

> *(GARROWAY is reaching into the pocket(s) of his coat – trying to retrieve his notebook.)*

**GARROWAY.** It's gone, sir.

**BEAMISH.** What's gone?

**GARROWAY.** My poem. I wrote it in my notebook and my notebook was in my pocket – and now it's gone.

**BEAMISH.** Then what is that in your hand?

**GARROWAY.** *(The stock certificate.)* Oh, that's a little investment I just made. The Finer and Better Motion Picture Company –

**BEAMISH.** – of Hollywood, California.

**GARROWAY.** You know it?

**BEAMISH.** How many shares?

**GARROWAY.** Thousands of dollars-worth!

**BEAMISH.** And you paid?

**GARROWAY.** Only three hundred bucks.

**BEAMISH.** You've been stung.

**GARROWAY.** What?!

**BEAMISH.** Does NO ONE READ THE PAPERS?! Garroway: that motion picture company is no longer in motion. They're dead and gone. The stock is nothing but waste paper.

**GARROWAY.** Ughghghghghghghghghgh.

(**GARROWAY** *is seething, pacing.*)

**BEAMISH.** Who sold it to you?

**GARROWAY.** I didn't get his name! But there'll be NOTHIN' LEFT OF HIM when I find him!

(**GARROWAY** *rushes off.*)

## The Garden of an Estate. Day.

(*A long gift table sits prominently at center.*)

*(SIGSBEE approaches FANNY – who stands away from the table, near some tall bushes. SIGSBEE is dressed for the wedding.)*

**SIGSBEE.** There you are – my silky-fingered pearl poacher!

**FANNY.** You said there'd been a change in plan.

**SIGSBEE.** You bet your thievin' knees there has: I convinced them to place the gift table *outside*. You will hide here, in these bushes, till the ceremony starts – and then lay a little larceny on us!

**FANNY.** And where will that pearl necklace be?

**SIGSBEE.** I've told Ferris to place it directly in the center of the table. I'll meet you right here after the ceremony – you'll give me the necklace, I'll give you your money, and we'll all live snappily ever after.

**FANNY.** You're wearing a boutonniere.

**SIGSBEE.** *(Proudly.)* I'm the father of the bride.

**FANNY.** That's awful! Stealing your own daughter's necklace –

**SIGSBEE.** Say, listen –

**FANNY.** – why would you do a thing like that?

**SIGSBEE.** *Never you mind, missy.* Into the bushes!

*(FANNY vanishes into the bushes, just as –)*

*(FINCH enters. He is dressed for the wedding, his mood buoyant.)*

**FINCH.** Hello, Mister Waddington!

**SIGSBEE.** Call me Sigsbee!

**FINCH.** All right, Sigsbee!

**SIGSBEE.** Oh, what the heck: call me "Dad."

**FINCH.** All right, *Dad.*

**SIGSBEE.** And I'll call you –

> (*Trying to remember.*)

*Whatever comes to mind.* Ready for the big day?

**FINCH.** I rose with the sun and stepped outside – where the birds were standing in the trees, singing Mendelssohn's "Wedding March" – all for Molly and me!

**SIGSBEE.** Birds love trees, all right. And bushes. They like bushes, too – scattered about, *strategic*, perfect for *hiding.*

**FINCH.** I don't think I follow you...

**SIGSBEE.** Seen anybody?

**FINCH.** Where?

**SIGSBEE.** *In the bushes?*

**FINCH.** No – I don't believe I have.

**SIGSBEE.** SEE THAT! It's PERFECT. HUP-HIP-HOODLEE-DOO!!!

> (*And* **SIGSBEE** *is gone, as –*)

> (**BEAMISH** *enters, opposite. He, too, is dressed for the wedding. He, too, is full of joy.*)

**BEAMISH.** And here is the lucky groom! Oh, what a day!

**FINCH.** You can say that again!

**BEAMISH.** I can and I will: What a day, George! What a day to be ME!

**FINCH.** Pardon?

**BEAMISH.** And YOU, of course, what a day to be you, as well – but I've just had the most wonderful news. My three week wait has ended. My beloved Eulalie is taking the train *directly here to the wedding.* Isn't that grand?

**FINCH.** What a day it will be!

**BEAMISH.** Speaking of which: there's been a slight hitch.

**FINCH.** What hitch and how slight?

**BEAMISH.** We've had a call from the clergyman. Early this morning, as he attempted to stand on a stool and reach down a volume of devotional thought –

**FINCH.** Yes?

**BEAMISH.** He fell.

**FINCH.** Poor man.

**BEAMISH.** And sprained his ankle.

**FINCH.** Poor fellow.

**BEAMISH.** And therefore cannot perform the service.

**FINCH.** The clumsy oaf!

**BEAMISH.** Don't worry, George. The necessary steps have been taken.

**FINCH.** No, in fact, the *UN*NECESSARY STEPS have been taken! Taken by this dumb-footed, errant climbing, stool-stumbling –

**BEAMISH.** George, calm yourself: another clergyman has been found. He's on his way up from Flushing.

**FINCH.** Oh, no.

**BEAMISH.** You don't approve of Flushing?

**FINCH.** I fear it's a bad portent. What if it means terrible things for the wedding?!

**BEAMISH.** It means nothing of the sort.

> (**FERRIS** *appears. He carries the gift box containing the pearl necklace. He places it in the center of the table.*)

**FERRIS.** Mister Finch, you've had a call from a young lady. She is coming here immediately.

**FINCH.** *(Offhand.)* Fine. Whatever.

**FERRIS.** Stubbs, sir. That is her name. May Stubbs.

(**FINCH** *freezes, as –*)

(**FERRIS** *goes.*)

**FINCH.** Oh, no. Oh, no. Oh, no. Oh, no. Oh, no.

**BEAMISH.** George, what is it?

**FINCH.** It's all the fault of that clergyman! He has rained this bad luck down upon me!

**BEAMISH.** Who is this May Stubbs?

**FINCH.** I knew her back in Idaho. We were *sort of engaged.*

**BEAMISH.** I fail to see how one can be *sort of engaged.*

**FINCH.** In East Gilead we have what are called "understandings." You see a girl home once or twice from church – have a few dinners at her parents' house – and, well, it's sort of assumed –

**BEAMISH.** – that you will marry her.

**FINCH.** And now May has read about my wedding to Molly, and is coming here to ruin it all.

**BEAMISH.** You really think so?

**FINCH.** What other reason could she have?

**BEAMISH.** None. You're doomed.

**FINCH.** There must be *something* I can do!

**BEAMISH.** Yes – something *revolting!*

**FINCH.** *What?*

**BEAMISH.** To make her renounce you forever. This May Stubbs – has she ever been to New York?

**FINCH.** Not that I know of.

**BEAMISH.** And is she rather straight-laced? *Prudish?*

**FINCH.** I never put her in a position to find out.

**BEAMISH.** No, I'm sure you didn't. But many of these small town girls are innocent to the ways of the world. Don't you see: we must lead her to believe that you have become a reprobate.

**FINCH.** A what?!

**BEAMISH.** A *Don Juan*, a *Lothario*, a *libertine*! I can see it now: Miss Stubbs is sitting next to you on a bench – a dowdy little thing in her gingham dress and lace-up shoes. And THEN – suddenly – before your eyes: a WOMAN APPEARS. A BAD woman. A *REAL BAD* woman – with black stockings and come-hither hair – that pensive and pallid face – those pouty, put-upon lips. And from those lips, the words begin to pour out:

*(Acting it out.)*

GEORGE FINCH, YOU DESERTED ME! LEFT ME COLD AND ALONE AND WITHOUT A WORD OF GOODBYE! YOU PROMISED TO MAKE *ME* YOUR WIFE – ME AND ME ALONE!

*(Beat. **FINCH** considers this.)*

**FINCH.** Oh, no. Oh, no. Oh, no. Oh, no. Oh, no.

**BEAMISH.** Have it your way. I'm only trying to help.

**FINCH.** Where would you find her, anyway?! This Woman in Black?

**BEAMISH.** You're right. That is a problem.

**FINCH.** I'm doomed.

**BEAMISH.** Poor George. If only you had a dark past.

**FINCH.** I fear my dark past is all ahead of me.

(**FINCH** *leaves.*)

(**BEAMISH** *starts to leave, opposite, when he catches sight of –*)

(**FANNY**, *emerging from the bushes. She looks around, then coolly moves near the gift table and stands behind it, facing us.*)

(**BEAMISH**, *too, moves in – unseen by* **FANNY** *– until he is standing behind her.* **FANNY** *reaches down and lifts the small gift box containing the pearls, just as* **BEAMISH** *says:*)

**BEAMISH**. Set.

(**FANNY** *freezes, caught.*)

The gift. Down.

(*She does so. Turns to him. They stare at each other.*)

Well? What do you have to say for yourself?

(*A beat. She takes a deep breath. And then, speaks with passion –*)

**FANNY**. (*In a thick Irish brogue.*) DON'T TURN ME OVER TO THE BULLS, MISTER! I ONLY DID IT FOR MY DEAR OLD MA! IF YOU WAS COLD AND STARVIN' AND HAD TO WATCH YOUR POOR OLD MA BENDIN' O'ER THE WASHTUB DAY AND NIGHT –!

**BEAMISH**. Wrong-wrong-wrong-wrong-wrong. Do you really think this crude Broadway melodrama will persuade a man of my worldly expertise?

**FANNY**. (*Drops the role.*) I thought, what the heck? – it's worth a try.

**BEAMISH**. Are you an actress?

**FANNY.** No, sir. I'm a thief. I love the theatre – but my parents didn't want me to fall in with the wrong crowd.

**BEAMISH.** You are not without dramatic ability.

**FANNY.** Really?

> (**BEAMISH** *is now scribbling with a pen onto his handkerchief.*)

**BEAMISH.** I think the Average Man – the Simple Man – the Unenlightened *Hoi Polloi* could, in fact, be swayed by you.

**FANNY.** *Huh?*

**BEAMISH.** I need a Wronged Woman.

**FANNY.** Look around – they're *everywhere.*

**BEAMISH.** My friend is to be married today. And when his previous fiancée arrives to make trouble, I need a Wronged Woman to step forward and play the role of my friend's discarded victim.

**FANNY.** *(Waffling.)* Oh, I don't know...

**BEAMISH.** Your choice: a moment on stage, or a month in the slammer.

**FANNY.** *(Immediately eager.)* Okay, what do I do?

**BEAMISH.** You will hide here, in these bushes. When my friend approaches with his bride-to-be, you will rush toward him and deliver a speech. I've written it on this handkerchief.

**FANNY.** *(Impressed.)* You mean a *"so-lil-o-key"?*

> (*He gives her the handkerchief.*)

**BEAMISH.** Take your place. They'll be here soon.

**FANNY.** What if they ask me questions?

**BEAMISH.** They won't. Because as soon as you have finished your speech, you will *collapse upon the gift table.* You will shout: MY PILLS! MY PILLS! I MUST HAVE MY PILLS! – and then you'll run away and be gone.

**FANNY.** Oh, I like that part about the pills.

**BEAMISH.** Okay, now –

**FANNY.** And the rushing out. That's called an *exit*, you know.

**BEAMISH.** As for your clothing –

**FANNY.** *(Quickly.) Costume.*

**BEAMISH.** – we'll need something a little more...

**FANNY.** Refined?

**BEAMISH.** Lurid. Nasty. Worthy of a brothel.

**FANNY.** Oh, I have just the thing! I stopped by *la French Boutique* on the way out of town – and I lifted a bit of lingerie for my honeymoon.

**BEAMISH.** Is it trashy?

**FANNY.** *Oui-oui.*

**BEAMISH.** That will be perfect. Now: into the bushes.

**FANNY.** *(As she goes.)* That's called *offstage.*

*(She vanishes once again, as –)*

*(**FINCH** appears, opposite – a nervous wreck.)*

**FINCH.** No sign of the minister from Flushing! And May Stubbs to arrive any minute!

**BEAMISH.** Calm yourself, George. Our plan is in place.

**FINCH.** But how?!

**BEAMISH.** No time to explain. But you must have Ferris guard the gift table. There are *thieves* about.

**FINCH.** Thieves? How do you know?

**BEAMISH.** Just do as I say, George – and all will be fine.

> (**BEAMISH** *goes, as –*)

> (**FERRIS** *enters, bringing a few final gifts to the table.*)

**FINCH.** He's done it, Ferris. The day is saved! Now, I have it on good authority that there are thieves lurking about.

**FERRIS.** Thieves, sir?

**FINCH.** Yes...they're...*drawn to the bushes*. You must guard the gift table, Ferris. At all costs.

> (**FERRIS** *produces a small tabloid newspaper – the* Tattler *– and reads, with interest.*)

> (**FINCH** *stands next to him.*)

Nice day.

**FERRIS.** Sir?

**FINCH.** Today. Very nice.

**FERRIS.** The weather appears to be clement, yes.

**FINCH.** And the countryside – just lovely. Don't you think?

**FERRIS.** No, sir.

**FINCH.** You don't approve of the country around here?

**FERRIS.** Not at all, sir.

**FINCH.** Why is that?

**FERRIS.** It is not England, sir.

> (**FERRIS** *reads.*)

(**FINCH** *looks at his watch.*)

**FINCH.** I see you read the *Tattler.*

**FERRIS.** Yes, sir.

**FINCH.** That paper is filled with nothing but the most outrageous gossip.

**FERRIS.** Indeed, it is.

**FINCH.** And you enjoy that?

**FERRIS.** Very much, sir.

(**FERRIS** *continues to read.*)

**FINCH.** Well, I hope you enjoy weddings, Ferris!

**FERRIS.** Weddings strike me as the most melancholy occasions imaginable.

**FINCH.** Of all things to say to me...

**FERRIS.** I was married. It ended. Like *all things do.* Ended fast and bitterly. Soon after the ceremony our love withered away like a brittle leaf on a dying tree. Our wedding, as it turned out, did not prolong our love. It merely *mummified the corpse.*

Will that be all, sir?

(**FINCH** *stares at* **FERRIS,** *aghast, as –*)

(**SIGSBEE** *arrives.*)

**SIGSBEE.** Ferris, I need a drink.

**FERRIS.** I'm presently occupied, sir.

**SIGSBEE.** Doing what?

**FERRIS.** Guarding the gift table.

**SIGSBEE.** *Why would you do something like that?*

**FERRIS.** There are thieves about. "Drawn to the bushes."

**SIGSBEE.** According to who?

**FERRIS.** Mister Finch.

**FINCH.** *(Waves.)* Hello, Dad.

**SIGSBEE.** I'll *DAD* you right down on your dusty *derriere!*

> **(MRS. WADDINGTON** *enters, dressed in black.)*

**MRS. WADDINGTON.** Well, another terrible thing has happened.

**FINCH.** What now?!

**MRS. WADDINGTON.** The minister from Flushing –

**FINCH.** Yes?!

**MRS. WADDINGTON.** – is able and willing to marry you. I *begged* the man to stand on a stool, but no such luck. What's more: it's his last wedding.

**FINCH.** He's leaving the Church?

**MRS. WADDINGTON.** He's leaving the country. On his new yacht. Sailing away to Bora Bora – rich as the day is long. He just made a killing in the market. Bought a thousand shares of some motion picture company out West.

**SIGSBEE.** *What did you say?*

**MRS. WADDINGTON.** The Better and Finer –

**SIGSBEE.** *(Correcting her.) Finer and Better –*

**MRS. WADDINGTON.** – Motion Picture Company of California.

**SIGSBEE.** That thing's a loser! They never made a picture!

**MRS. WADDINGTON.** No, they didn't. But, when a workman dug a hole on the lot to put up a "For Sale" sign – *he struck oil*. It's the biggest gusher in the southwest.

*(To* **SIGSBEE**, *sharp.)*

**MRS. WADDINGTON.** Why can't you ever buy a stock like that?!

**SIGSBEE.** *(Desperate.)* When did this happen?

**MRS. WADDINGTON.** Just this morning. It's not even in the papers, yet.

*(And* **SIGSBEE** *bolts away, saying –)*

**SIGSBEE.** Then there's still time to get it back! – *GALLAGHER – GALLAHAD – GARRITY!*

**MRS. WADDINGTON.** Ferris, I need a drink.

**FERRIS.** I'm occupied, Madame. Guarding the gift table. At Mister Finch's directive.

**MRS. WADDINGTON.** Only an imbecile would suggest such a thing.

**FERRIS.** *Precisely*, Madame.

*(***MS. WADDINGTON** *and* **FERRIS** *exit, as –)*

**FINCH.** But, Ferris –

*(***BEAMISH** *and* **MADAME EULALIE** *enter, arm in arm.)*

**BEAMISH.** And I think I've told you about my friend George Finch.

**MADAME EULALIE.** The lucky groom-to-be.

*(Upon seeing* **MADAME EULALIE, FINCH** *freezes.)*

**BEAMISH.** I'm afraid George is a bit shell-shocked. An old flame of his has threatened to turn up today and stop the wedding. A dowdy little thing named May Stubbs.

**MADAME EULALIE.** What an awful name.

**BEAMISH.** Not to worry: I've arranged a *little drama* that will make her renounce him forever.

**MADAME EULALIE.** Hamilton Beamish: you are too clever for one man. You ought to incorporate.

**BEAMISH.** George, can you say hello? This is Lalie. And this is her smile. And this is her hair. And this is her dress – a dress that must have been *cut by fairy scissors out of moonbeams and stardust...*

**MADAME EULALIE.** Hello, George.

**FINCH.** Hello, May.

> (**BEAMISH** *turns to* **MADAME EULALIE** – *then to* **FINCH** – *then back to* **MADAME EULALIE**.)

**BEAMISH.** *May?*

**MADAME EULALIE.** Yes, I'm the dowdy little thing.

**BEAMISH.** You're not a dowdy little thing.

**MADAME EULALIE.** I was when George knew me. Back in East Gilead.

**BEAMISH.** But your name is Madame Eulalie.

**MADAME EULALIE.** Much better than May Stubbs, don't you think?

> (*To* **FINCH**.)

How've you been, George? I never heard from you.

**FINCH.** May, listen – it was just one of those youthful things.

**MADAME EULALIE.** Oh, was it really?

**FINCH.** You don't really think I'm engaged to you –

**MADAME EULALIE.** Why wouldn't I? After the letters you wrote.

**BEAMISH.** *Letters?*

**FINCH.** May, listen –

**MADAME EULALIE.** The way you'd sit with me for hours, on the sofa in the parlour.

**BEAMISH.** *The parlour?*

**FINCH.** May, please –

**MADAME EULALIE.** And the way my little brother would call you April Showers. Do you remember why?

**FINCH.** Because I brought May flowers.

**MADAME EULALIE.** Yes, you did, George. We had an *understanding.*

**FINCH.** Yes, I *know,* but –

**BEAMISH.** *(Transformed.)* WRONG-WRONG-WRONG-WRONG-*WRONG*. Now, you listen to me, George Finch: you are engaged to two of the loveliest women in the world. But when it comes to THIS ONE HERE you better just BACK AWAY before you GET BUSTED IN THE BEEZER! *One*: I LOVE HER, see?! *Two*: she's going to MARRY ME, see?! And, *Three*: anyone who says different had better tell his pals where he wants the BODY SENT – because I'M THE GUY THEY'RE GONNA CALL "APRIL SHOWERS!" – I'M THE GUY THAT'S HITCHIN' MY WAGON TO THAT DREAMY MAY STUBBS!!!

**MADAME EULALIE.** Oh, Jimmy – do you mean it?

**BEAMISH.** We'll tie the knot tomorrow! That is...

> *(***BEAMISH** *goes down on one knee before her.)*

...if you'll have me?

**MADAME EULALIE.** *(Her fortune-teller voice.)* I see a beautiful future ahead.

> *(***MADAME EULALIE** *and* **BEAMISH** *embrace, as –)*

*(**MOLLY** enters in her wedding gown.)*

**FINCH.** Molly!

**MOLLY.** Hello, George!

**FINCH.** *(Shielding his eyes.)* Isn't this bad luck – to see you before the ceremony?

**MOLLY.** I don't believe in those silly superstitions. Do you?

**BEAMISH.** Miss Waddington, I'd like you to meet my fiancée.

| **MADAME EULALIE.** | **MOLLY.** |
|---|---|
| Congratulations! | Congratulations! |

**BEAMISH.** She was once engaged to George!

*(**MOLLY** turns to **GEORGE**.)*

**MADAME EULALIE.** We had an *understanding.*

**BEAMISH.** It was *years ago.*

**MADAME EULALIE.** *In Idaho.*

**MOLLY.** George. Is that true?

**FINCH.** Ummmmmmmm...*yes.*

*(**MOLLY** now turns and looks at **MADAME EULALIE**.)*

**MOLLY.** Well, then. We are two of the luckiest women in the world.

*(**MADAME EULALIE** smiles, and **MOLLY** takes her hand.)*

**FINCH.** So, you're not jealous?

**MOLLY.** I know you love me, George. And because I know that, I could never be jealous.

*(**MRS. WADDINGTON** and **FERRIS** enter.)*

**MRS. WADDINGTON.** Ferris, tell them the bad news.

**FERRIS.** The minister is ready to perform the service.

| **MOLLY.** | **MADAME EULALIE & BEAMISH.** |
|---|---|
| Wonderful! | Hooray! |

**FINCH.** (*To* **MRS. WADDINGTON.**) After you, Mother.

> (**MRS. WADDINGTON** *glares at* **FINCH,** *as* **MADAME EULALIE** *takes* **BEAMISH**'s *arm.*)

**MADAME EULALIE.** I guess you won't need your "little drama" after all.

**BEAMISH.** What's that?

> (*Instantly remembers.*)

*Oh, my.*

> (*And in rushes* **FANNY.** *She wears a perfectly trashy black and red negligée, fish net stockings, high heels, the works. She carries the handkerchief, reading from it – playing her role brilliantly.*)

**FANNY.** GEORGE FINCH, YOU DESERTED ME!

**FINCH.** *Who are you?*

**BEAMISH.** No, STOP!

**FANNY.** LEFT ME COLD AND ALONE AND WITHOUT A WORD OF GOODBYE!

**MRS. WADDINGTON.** IT'S JUST LIKE IN THE CRYSTAL BALL!

**FANNY.** YOU PROMISED TO MAKE ME YOUR WIFE – ME AND ME ALONE!!!

| **BEAMISH.** | **MOLLY.** |
|---|---|
| That's ENOUGH! | George? – WHO IS THIS?! |

**FINCH.** Molly – I CAN EXPLAIN –

**FANNY.** *(A cry.)* AAAAAAAAAHHHHHHHHHH!

> (**FANNY** *tosses the handkerchief and turns upstage – where she collapses upon the gift table for only a moment –)*

**MRS. WADDINGTON.** MOLLY, LOOK OUT – *SHE'S GOT A GUN!*

> *(– and then* **FANNY** *turns, with of course no gun in hand, and rushes away, saying –)*

**FANNY.** MY PILLS! MY PILLS! I MUST HAVE MY PILLS!!!

> (**FANNY** *vanishes into the bushes, as –)*

> (**BEAMISH** *hurriedly grabs the handkerchief and runs after her – joined in pursuit by* **MADAME EULALIE.***)*

**BEAMISH.** STOP – WAIT!

> (**FINCH** *turns to* **MOLLY.***)*

**FINCH.** Molly – please...it's not what you think.

> *(But* **MOLLY** *has turned and stormed away –)*

Molly!

> *(– As* **MRS. WADDINGTON** *announces, victoriously:)*

**MRS. WADDINGTON.** SEND THAT MINISTER HOME!

## Sigsbee Waddington's Study. The Next Morning.

(**SIGSBEE** *limps into the room, and collapses in his chair. He still wears his clothes from the night before – now completely disheveled.*)

(**FERRIS** *follows him with a stiff drink on a tray.*)

(**SIGSBEE** *takes off his cowboy boots and rubs his feet.*)

**SIGSBEE.** Oh, my achin' dogs! – I must have walked every sidewalk in the whole blasted city!

**FERRIS.** Your drink, sir.

**SIGSBEE.** There I am, halfway to Pennsylvania Station when it dawns on me that the fellow's name isn't *Garrity*, at all – his name is *Mulcahy. Do you have any idea how many cops there are in New York City named Mulcahy?*! But not ONE of 'em was the one I wanted – and now here I am – no stock in hand – about to be *DRAWN AND QUARTERED for missing my own daughter's wedding!*

**FERRIS.** There was no wedding, sir.

**SIGSBEE.** What?!

**FERRIS.** A Wronged Woman appeared and impugned the integrity of Mister Finch.

**SIGSBEE.** And where is this woman now?

**FERRIS.** After collapsing upon the gift table, she vanished into the bushes.

(*Beat.*)

**SIGSBEE.** The *gift table*, you say?

**FERRIS.** Yes, sir.

**SIGSBEE.** The *bushes*, you say?

**FERRIS.** Yes, sir.

**SIGSBEE**. Holy artichokes of Jerusalem!

**FERRIS**. Pardon me, sir?

**SIGSBEE**. Where are the gifts, Ferris?

**FERRIS**. They were brought back this morning. Unopened.

**SIGSBEE**. Do you remember the small gift I asked you to place in the center of the table?

**FERRIS**. Yes, sir.

**SIGSBEE**. Bring it to me, Ferris – right this instant!

(**FERRIS** *goes.*)

Great Godfrey in Havana! – it's my lucky day!

(**MRS. WADDINGTON** *appears.* **MOLLY** *is with her, angry and glum.*)

**MRS. WADDINGTON**. Might I just say that P. Homer Horlick would never have run out on his own daughter's wedding.

**SIGSBEE**. First of all, I know there was no wedding. And what's more, Molly: *it's not what you think.*

**MOLLY**. George said the same thing.

(**FERRIS** *arrives with the gift.*)

**SIGSBEE**. (*To* **MOLLY**.) I want you to open this gift.

| **MOLLY**. | **MRS. WADDINGTON**. |
|---|---|
| Papa, please... | Is this some kind of cruel *joke?* |

**SIGSBEE**. Not at all. In that box is the pearl necklace you were promised. Go on: take a look.

(**MOLLY** *opens the box.*)

**MOLLY**. It's empty.

**SIGSBEE.** Bingo!

**MOLLY.** It's gone! – my necklace –

**SIGSBEE.** It was all a "set-up job." Don't you see? That was no Wronged Woman! That person was a THIEF. And when she fell on the gift table – she stole the pearl necklace – and then vanished into the bushes!

**MOLLY.** You mean, George didn't even *know her*?

**SIGSBEE.** Certainly not.

**MOLLY.** You mean, George is innocent after all!

| **SIGSBEE.** | **MRS. WADDINGTON.** |
|---|---|
| He certainly IS! | Oh, no he's NOT! |

**MOLLY.** I need to find him and apologize.

**MRS. WADDINGTON.** I will not allow you to visit the home of known LIBERTINE who plays the UKULELE!

**MOLLY.** He does NOT play the UKULELE!

(*And* **MOLLY** *is gone.*)

**MRS. WADDINGTON.** (*Calling off.*) MOLLY.

**SIGSBEE.** I need to find that policeman!

**MRS. WADDINGTON.** You will NOT go the police! If word of this got to the *Tattler* – we'd be the laughing stock of New York, wouldn't we Ferris?

**FERRIS.** Indeed, you would.

(**SIGSBEE** *has put on his boots and is rushing out –*)

**SIGSBEE.** What was his name? Carradine – Gaberdine – Ovaltine –

**MRS. WADDINGTON.** SIGSBEE.

(*But he, too, is gone.*)

FERRIS.

**FERRIS**.  Yes, Madame?

**MRS. WADDINGTON**.  *(Seething.)* Prepare the car.

**FERRIS**.  I wonder, Madame, if I might ride downtown with you. I've had a call from an Uncle near Sheridan Square. He is ill and I wish to visit him.

**MRS. WADDINGTON**.  Oh, very well. Just keep this out of the *Tattler*.

> (**MRS. WADDINGTON** *goes, as –)*

> (**FERRIS** *steps into an area of light which will serve as a –)*

## Street Corner. Day.

> (**FERRIS** *stops* **GARROWAY**, *who is walking past – holding the worthless stock certificate.)*

**FERRIS**.  Pardon me, bobby.

**GARROWAY**.  I'm not Bobby.

**FERRIS**.  I'm sorry. I mistook you for a policeman.

**GARROWAY**.  I am a policeman.

**FERRIS**.  Very good, bobby. Now: I'm looking for the office of J. Lancelot Biffin.

**GARROWAY**.  The publisher of the *Tattler*?

**FERRIS**.  Yes.

**GARROWAY**.  He's on the fifth floor. Right across the hall from Mister Beamish.

**FERRIS**.  Thank you, bobby.

**GARROWAY**.  *My name is not –*

**FERRIS**.  Cheerio!

## Office of the "Tattler." Afternoon.

*(FERRIS sits, typing away on a typewriter. As he does so, we occasionally hear the VOICE OF J. LANCELOT BIFFIN from an adjacent (unseen) room. He speaks with a British accent.)*

**VOICE OF BIFFIN.** IT BETTER BE GOOD, FERRIS. GOOD AND NASTY.

**FERRIS.** The readers of the *Tattler* shan't be disappointed, Mister Biffin! I shall call it: "THE WICKED WORLD OF THE WADDINGTONS."

**VOICE OF BIFFIN.** I WANT LOTS OF STUFF ABOUT THAT WOMAN IN BLACK.

**FERRIS.** Not a single lurid detail shall be omitted!

**VOICE OF BIFFIN.** GOOD MAN.

**FERRIS.** I so admire the *Tattler,* Mister Biffin. It makes me long for England: where a vicious little tabloid can *bring the Royals to their knees!*

**VOICE OF BIFFIN.** KEEP AN EYE OUT, FERRIS – EVERYONE'S HUNGRY TO STEAL A GOOD SCOOP.

**FERRIS.** Yes, sir.

*(MRS. WADDINGTON appears behind him, out of breath.)*

**MRS. WADDINGTON.** Pardon me, sir – I'm sorry to intrude, but I'm looking for the apartment of George Finch, the *bohemian artist and scoundrel!*

**FERRIS.** *(Not having seen her face.)* You're too late, Buster – whoever you are. The SCOOP is MINE.

**MRS. WADDINGTON.** Ferris!

**FERRIS.** *(Turns.)* Mrs. Waddington!

    *(Instantly calm.)*

Good afternoon.

**MRS. WADDINGTON.** What are you doing?

**FERRIS.** Visiting my sick Uncle.

**MRS. WADDINGTON.** But what are you typing?

**FERRIS.** His Last Will and Testament.

**VOICE OF BIFFIN.** HURRY UP, FERRIS.

**FERRIS.** *(Calling off.)* Nearly finished.

**VOICE OF BIFFIN.** I HAVEN'T MUCH TIME.

**FERRIS.** *(To* **MRS. WADDINGTON.***)* Poor man. He's *quite ill.*

**MRS. WADDINGTON.** Well, I'm sorry to hear that – but I've come to catch Mister Finch *in flagrante delicto,* and I need YOU to be there as my witness!

**FERRIS.** *(Interested now.)* Very good, Madame! I'll include it as a sequel.

**MRS. WADDINGTON.** A *sequel to his will?*

**FERRIS.** You run along and find Mister Finch. I'll join you shortly.

**MRS. WADDINGTON.** But –

**VOICE OF BIFFIN.** TIME'S UP, FERRIS. I'M GOING NOW.

**FERRIS.** *(To* **MRS. WADDINGTON.***)* As you can see: I really must finish up.

    *(He returns to his typing, as –)*

    *(***MRS. WADDINGTON*** leaves and lights shift to –)*

## The Roof. Day.

(**MULLETT** *is pacing, troubled, as –*)

(**FANNY** *enters from the apartment. She is wearing a sheer robe over the negligée we saw earlier. She holds a very large pot of pepper.*)

**FANNY.** Pookee, what is it? What's wrong?

**MULLETT.** I waited up half the night for you, Fanny. I want to know where you were.

**FANNY.** It's where I *AM* that matters: I'm *right here.* With my dear husband. Making a nice rabbit stew.

(*Close to him.*)

Okay, Pookee?

**MULLETT.** (*Beginning to relent.*) Did you remember the pepper?

**FANNY.** Of course I did. I know how you love pepper in your stew.

(*Takes his hand, winks.*) Now – let me check the stew – and then we'll go stir the pot!

(**FANNY** *and* **MULLETT** *exit into the apartment, just as –*)

(**MOLLY,** *now dressed in "bohemian attire," emerges from the stairwell, and –*)

(**MRS. WADDINGTON** *emerges from the fire escape.*)

| MOLLY. | MRS. WADDINGTON. |
|---|---|
| Mother! | Molly! |

**MOLLY.** *(Continued.)* What are you *doing here?*

**MRS. WADDINGTON.** Never mind that. What are you *wearing?*

**MOLLY.** I'm one of THEM, now, Mother. I'm a BOHEMIAN!

**MRS. WADDINGTON.** But, I just saw you at home an hour ago!

**MOLLY.** *Art is fast, Mother.* Now – out of my way.

> *(She heads towards Finch's apartment, as* **MRS. WADDINGTON** *tries to stop her –)*

**MRS. WADDINGTON.** I will not let you see that scoundrel.

**MOLLY.** I'm marrying him, Mother – no matter what you say. *Nothing* can stop me now.

**MRS. WADDINGTON.** But, Molly –

**MOLLY.** George Finch is the most dear, the most decent, the most honest –

> *(***FANNY** *– in her negligée and robe – rushes out the door of the apartment on her way to the sleeping porch. She does not see the other women.)*

**FANNY.** C'mon, sweetie pie! – I know how long you've waited!

> *(***FANNY** *vanishes into the sleeping porch and shuts the door.)*

**MOLLY.** *(Fully changed.)* – the most *conniving*, the most *deceitful*, the most *despicable man I've ever known!* *He's TAKEN HER BACK! It's TRUE – it's ALL TRUE!*

> *(***MOLLY** *rushes out the stairwell, as –)*

(**MRS. WADDINGTON** *marches with across the roof and pounds on the door of the apartment.*)

(**MULLETT** *throws open the door, saying –*)

**MULLETT.** I'm comin', Pookee!

**MRS. WADDINGTON.** I am not your *pookee*. Now: who was that woman flouncing across the roof?

**MULLETT.** That woman was my wife.

**MRS. WADDINGTON.** Mister Finch is sleeping with your wife?!

**MULLETT.** *I beg your pardon?!*

**MRS. WADDINGTON.** Get out of my way – I'll question him myself!

**MULLETT.** Mister Finch is not here.

**MRS. WADDINGTON.** Then I wish to question his man-servant.

**MULLETT.** That's exactly what you're doing.

**MRS. WADDINGTON.** How long have you worked for Mister Finch?

**MULLETT.** Since I got out of prison.

**MRS. WADDINGTON.** Does he have girls up here?

**MULLETT.** All the time.

**MRS. WADDINGTON.** Scantily-clad little things, I bet.

**MULLETT.** No, ma'am – they're *nude. Completely nude.*

**MRS. WADDINGTON.** Aha!

**MULLETT.** They *pose* for him – he's an ARTIST, you know!

**MRS. WADDINGTON.** Oh, don't I know!

*(And she slams the door on* **MULLETT** *and heads for the stairwell –)*

MOLLY!

*(– While at the same time,* **GARROWAY** *emerges from the stairwell, heading for the apartment –)*

**GARROWAY**. MULLETT!

*(Seeing a policeman,* **MRS. WADDINGTON** *hides behind the door as* **GARROWAY** *opens it.)*

*(***GARROWAY*** pounds on the door to the apartment.)*

*(***MULLETT*** throws open the door, saying –)*

**MULLETT**. Lady, I'm on my HONEYMOON!

**GARROWAY**. Congratulations. Now, listen: I need the name of the old trickster who swindled me out of three hundred bucks. *I met him on this roof.*

**MULLETT**. I haven't seen him.

**GARROWAY**. I think he stole my poetry notebook, too!

**MULLETT**. But I have seen an *intruder.*

**GARROWAY**. *(Instantly interested.)* You don't say.

**MULLETT**. Some clever old bag, prowling about on the roof. If I were you, I'd pinch her on suspicion.

**GARROWAY**. Thanks for the tip, Mullett – but I'm due down at the Station. Tonight's the night we're raiding the Purple Chicken!

*(***MRS. WADDINGTON*** emerges from behind the stairwell door and disappears inside the apartment, just as –)*

**FANNY'S VOICE.**  *(From the sleeping porch.) POOKEE!*

**MULLETT.**  I gotta run.

> *(From the apartment: the sound of pots and pans falling.* **GARROWAY** *readies his nightstick, and approaches. He knocks on the door, then hides near the wall, as –)*

> *(***MRS. WADDINGTON** *opens the door. She is holding the large pot of pepper.)*

> *(***GARROWAY** *jumps out and surprises her –)*

**GARROWAY.**  You're pinched!

> *(– And* **MRS. WADDINGTON** *tosses the full contents of the pepper-pot into* **GARROWAY**'s *face.)*

> *(He stumbles about and immediately begins sneezing uncontrollably –)*

*AAAAAAAAAHHHHHHH! THTOP! THIEF! THOMBODY THTOP HER! AAAAAAAA-TCHOOOOOOO!!!*

> *(***MRS. WADDINGTON** *rushes down the fire escape, just as –)*

> *(***MOLLY** *emerges from the stairwell, heading for the apartment –)*

**MOLLY.**  Okay, George – it's time you heard a piece of my mind!

> *(– Where she encounters* **GARROWAY**.*)*

**GARROWAY.**  Aaatchooo!

**MOLLY.**  OH NO...

> *(A quick* **GARROWAY** *sneeze. A quick* **MOLLY** *realization.)*

Is GEORGE WANTED BY THE LAW?!

**GARROWAY.** ATHATHIN.

**MOLLY.** George is an ASSASSIN?!

**GARROWAY.** A *PEPPER-POT ATHATHIN.* STHE THWARTED ME WITH LETHAL STHPICES!

**MOLLY.** Wait – are you talking about *my* George?

> (**GARROWAY** *shakes his head "NO" – as he sneezes.*)

Or that WOMAN WHO WAS HERE?

> (**GARROWAY** *nods "YES" – as he sneezes.*)

I knew it! She was young, wasn't she?

**GARROWAY.** Old.

**MOLLY.** Red hair.

**GARROWAY.** Grey.

**MOLLY.** Tall.

**GARROWAY.** Thhort.

**MOLLY.** Slender.

**GARROWAY.** Thtout.

**MOLLY.** A real salty wench.

**GARROWAY.** No, ma'am: it wath *pepper.* Aaatchooo!

**MOLLY.** *(Her heart sinking again.)* Well, whoever she was – it means my Georgie is a scoundrel, just like Mother said.

**GARROWAY.** LITHEN: Thith wath no *thex kitten!* – thith wath a *burglar* – cathing out the plath!

**MOLLY.** A *burglar?*

**GARROWAY.** Oh, yeth, ma'am.

**MOLLY.** I've got to find George and apologize. And you've got to help me. I'd like to report a missing person: his name is Finch. George Fi –

**GARROWAY.** Thorry, ma'am – but I've got to get drethed. I'm part of the *undercover pothee* thath going to RAID THE PURPLE CHICKEN.

(*He races off down the stairwell –*)

**MOLLY.** But, I need your help!

(*– As the door to the sleeping porch opens slightly, revealing only the head of* **MULLETT**, *who is presumably otherwise unclothed.*)

**MULLETT.** Is something wrong, Miss?

**MOLLY.** *Who are you?* What are you doing in there?

**MULLETT.** Oh, just this and that.

(*A hand – presumably* **FANNY**'s *– pulls* **MULLETT**'s *head back inside the door, just as –*)

(**BEAMISH** *and* **MADAME EULALIE** *emerge from the apartment.*)

**MADAME EULALIE.** (*Seeing* **MOLLY**.) Jimmy – she's out here!

**BEAMISH.** Oh, Molly, I need to explain. That woman at the wedding – she was an actress.

**MOLLY.** No, she wasn't. She was a *thief.*

**BEAMISH.** Yes, I know, but perhaps with the proper training...

**MOLLY.** Mister Beamish, please: just help me find George.

**BEAMISH.** Lalie and I will go down to the Purple Chicken – they might have seen him down there.

(**BEAMISH** *and* **MADAME EULALIE** *are vanished into the stairwell.*)

**MOLLY.** *(Calling off.)* WAIT! – don't go there tonight – THE PURPLE CHICKEN IS GOING TO BE RAIDED!

### The Purple Chicken. Evening.

(**GARROWAY** *is seated at a table, wearing his foppish "Delancy Cabot" outfit from Act One. He is eating from a really huge pasta plate.*)

(**FINCH** *enters, alone and distraught, looking around for an empty table.*)

**FINCH.** Pardon me, sir. There's not a table to be found. Would you mind if I joined you?

**GARROWAY.** Not at all.

**FINCH.** *(As he sits.)* I've never seen the Purple Chicken this busy.

**GARROWAY.** It's a big night, all right. Aatchoo!

**FINCH.** Bless you.

*(Calling off, waving.)*

Hello, Giuseppe. Yes, today was the wedding – or rather *should have been* – I'd rather not discuss it. I'll have the *prix fixe* – *very light on the pepper*, if you would – with the clear soup, and, of course –

(**FINCH** *does a little "signal" here to signify he wants some booze.*)

Thanks, Giuseppe.

**GARROWAY.** They seem to know you here.

**FINCH.**  I live just up the fire escape.

    *(Extends his hand.)*

  George Finch.

**GARROWAY.**  Cabot. Delancy Cabot. I'm a poet.

**FINCH.**  And I'm an artist.

**GARROWAY.**  A pleasure.

**FINCH.**  Where do your poems appear?

**GARROWAY.**  I've never been published.

**FINCH.**  And I've never sold a picture.

**GARROWAY.**  Well, there you are.

**FINCH.**  It's a hard life, isn't it?

**GARROWAY.**  Stark.

**FINCH.**  A preacher falls from a stool and everything's ruined.

**GARROWAY.**  Grim.

**FINCH.**  And all that's left are the streets. It's all I've done for hours, you know. Walk those streets – lost and alone – those foul, dismal, perilous –

| **FINCH.** | **GARROWAY.** |
|---|---|
| *(Continued.)* – streets. | Streets! |

    **(FINCH** *leans in, considers* **GARROWAY** *for a moment.)*

**FINCH.**  *(Continued.)* I have an odd feeling that we've met before. Do you frequent the Chicken?

**GARROWAY.**  No, sir. Tonight's my first night.

**FINCH.**  But your face – it looks very familiar.

**GARROWAY.**  I have that kind of face.

**FINCH.** Well. You're kind to let me bend your ear. Perhaps you'll join me in a little...

*(He does the "signal".)*

**GARROWAY.** And by a little...

*(**GARROWAY** also does the "signal".)*

...you mean...?

**FINCH.** *(A whisper.)* A highball. Magic moonshine. A wicked little shot of hootch.

**GARROWAY.** Do you mean to say that a fellow can *get it here?*

**FINCH.** Of course you can! – if they know you – and they *absolutely know ME.* Whaddya say, will you help a fella drown his sorrows?

*(Calling off.)*

*GIUSEPPE!*

*(He does the "signal" again, impatiently – big enough for the whole restaurant to see.)*

**GARROWAY.** But isn't that against the law?

**FINCH.** *(From laughter to tears.)* Oh, Mr. Cabot, that's good – a poet with a sense of humor. You know what you should write a poem about? A man whose own valet, the good Mister Mullett, is away somewhere on his honeymoon – embedded with his Fanny in connubial bliss – while I sit here in a bootlegger's den, getting likkered up like a cowboy.

**GARROWAY.** Mullett is a good man.

**FINCH.** *You bet he is.* Despite what this meddling old policeman tried to tell me.

**GARROWAY.** And what was that?

**FINCH.**  This bonehead with a badge made it a point to tell me Mullett had been pinched for stealing.

**GARROWAY.**  You don't say.

**FINCH.**  That he'd been in prison at Sing Sing –

**GARROWAY.**  Really?

**FINCH.**  – and that, well...

> *(Beginning to realize.)*

...I think I'm beginning to remember where we met, sir.

> *(Calling off.)*

GIUSEPPE!

> *(He now gestures: "No. Stop. Don't Bring Me Any".)*

*(Calling off.)* I'LL HAVE MY USUAL GINGER-ALE! THANKS, GIUSEPPE!

> *(To* **GARROWAY**.*)*

I was kidding about the booze. Surely you knew that.

> *(***GARROWAY*** *stands and prepares his nightstick.)*

And my name is *not George Finch* – and I don't live *right upstairs* –

**GARROWAY.**  Tell it to the judge, buddy. Cause YOU'RE PINCHED.

> *(***GARROWAY*** *blows a loud whistle, as –)*

> *(***FINCH*** *throws the tablecloth up and over* **GARROWAY**'s *head.* **GARROWAY** *swings his nightstick – unable to see what's going on.* **FINCH** *takes the huge pasta bowl and smacks* **GARROWAY** *on the head.)*

(**FINCH** *drops the plate, turns to run and bumps headlong into –)*

(**SIGSBEE**, *who is marching through the restaurant, calling out –)*

**SIGSBEE.** Larrabee – Willoughby – Wallabee –

**FINCH.** Mr. Waddington!

**SIGSBEE.** Pinch, I need to find that policeman! I met him on your roof!

**FINCH.** Sorry – haven't seen him!

**GARROWAY.** *(Head still covered.)* STOP!

(**FINCH** *rushes out, and –)*

(**SIGSBEE** *rushes off, opposite, passing –)*

**SIGSBEE.** Wallabee – Wadderly – Waddington –!!!

(**BEAMISH** *and* **MADAME EULALIE** – *who are trying to get out of the restaurant – but instead bump headlong into* **GARROWAY**.)

**GARROWAY.** *(Head still covered, waving his nightstick.)* Grab him – grab that man!

**BEAMISH.** My god – it's a riot in here!

**MADAME EULALIE.** Where can we go?

**BEAMISH.** Follow me!

**GARROWAY.** I've been pummeled –

(**BEAMISH** *leads* **MADAME EULALIE** *away, as –)*

(**GARROWAY**'s *head finally emerges –)*

Pummeled with a pasta plate!

(*– But no one is there. He rushes off, nightstick poised, as lights shift quickly to –*)

## The Roof. Evening.

(**FINCH** *emerges from the fire escape. He runs toward his apartment, saying –*)

**FINCH.** Oh, no. Oh, no. Oh, no. Oh, no. Oh, no.

(*– While, at the same time, the door to the stairwell flies open and* **MRS. WADDINGTON** *appears, watching* **FINCH**.)

(**FINCH** *changes his mind – and races into the sleeping porch instead, slamming the door behind him.*)

**MRS. WADDINGTON.** He's at it again! MOLLY!

(*She slams the door to the stairwell, just as –*)

(**BEAMISH** *and* **MADAME EULALIE** *emerge from the fire escape.*)

**MADAME EULALIE.** (*Excitedly.*) Oh, Jimmy, we were nearly pinched –

**BEAMISH.** I shall never forgive myself –

**MADAME EULALIE.** Are you kidding? I loved it!

**BEAMISH.** (*Re: fire escape.*) They'll be right behind us – we've got to make a plan.

**MADAME EULALIE.** Down the stairwell?

**BEAMISH.** They'll have a man posted there.

**MADAME EULALIE.** Through George's apartment – we can take the elevator down to your place.

**BEAMISH.** Not with Lancelot Biffin right across the hall! We'll end up in the *Tattler* for sure.

**MADAME EULALIE.** *(With a wink.)* Would that be so wrong?

**BEAMISH.** I have it! *I'll* go down by way of the elevator. *You* go inside George's sleeping porch. Make yourself comfortable. When the police arrive, tell them Mister Finch rented you the place and that you're dressing to go to dinner. I shall appear in a few minutes – fully respectable – and inquire if you are ready to dine. How's that for a plan?

**MADAME EULALIE.** *It's the goods*, Jimmy.

**BEAMISH.** Really?

**MADAME EULALIE.** It's the *cracker jack* and the *ding-dong-king!*

**BEAMISH.** Might it even be considered *the bees knees?*

**MADAME EULALIE.** *You got it made, McDade!*

**BEAMISH.** OH, I LOVE TALKING THIS WAY.

    **(BEAMISH** *exits into the apartment, and –)*

    **(MADAME EULALIE** *enters –)*

### The Sleeping Porch. Evening.

    **(MADAME EULALIE** *stands just downstage of the bed. The only other object required in the room is a large wardrobe.)*

    **(MADAME EULALIE** *hums a little ditty to herself, as she puts on Fanny's robe – which was on the bed. Then, she kicks off her shoes. As the shoes fall to the ground –)*

(**FINCH**'s *head lifts the bed skirt and peeks out. He is staring at a pair of ankles. His eyes grow wide as moons.*)

(**MADAME EULALIE** *sits on the bed and reaches down to grab her shoes – and* **FINCH** *instinctively hands them to her. Realizing what he's done, he ducks under the bed before she suspects anything.*)

(*Meanwhile, back on –*)

## The Roof.

(**MRS. WADDINGTON** *has emerged from the stairwell – pulling* **MOLLY** *by the arm.*)

**MOLLY**.  Mother – let go of me!

**MRS. WADDINGTON**.  I'll show you once and for all! He's IN THERE WITH HER RIGHT NOW!

(**MRS. WADDINGTON** *pounds on the door to the sleeping porch.*)

**VOICE OF MADAME EULALIE**.  Who's there?

**MRS. WADDINGTON**.  Open this door!

**VOICE OF MADAME EULALIE**.  I'm dressing.

**MRS. WADDINGTON**.  *Undressing* is more like it – with Mister Finch watching you, I bet!

**MOLLY**.  Mother, you're wrong –

**VOICE OF MADAME EULALIE**.  There's no one here but me.

**MOLLY**.  Completely wrong about George –

**MRS. WADDINGTON**.  Listen, young lady – *I know the score now* –

*(A police whistle blows and* **MRS. WADDINGTON** *immediately shrieks –)*

Yikes!

*(– And rushes back into the stairwell, leaving* **MOLLY** *on the roof.)*

**MOLLY.** *Mother?!*

*(***GARROWAY*** *emerges from the fire escape, worse for fear – his foppish clothes are ripped and ruined. His policeman's hat is once again on his head. He heads toward the apartment –)*

Officer – what are you doing?!

**GARROWAY.** You told me to find "George Finch" and that's what I'm gonna do!

*(***GARROWAY*** *pounds on the apartment door.)*

**MOLLY.** He's not in there!

*(***GARROWAY*** *turns and heads toward the sleeping porch.)*

**GARROWAY.** I know he's up here somewhere – and when I find him, he's off to the slammer!

**MOLLY.** The slammer? – NO!

*(***GARROWAY*** *pounds on the sleeping porch door –)*

**VOICE OF MADAME EULALIE.** I told you: *I'm dressing.*

**GARROWAY.** Is George Finch is hiding in there?!

**VOICE OF MADAME EULALIE.** There's NO ONE HERE BUT ME!

**MOLLY.** *(To* **GARROWAY.***)* See – I told you!

(**GARROWAY** *now takes a few steps back and prepares to run and knock down the door.*)

**GARROWAY**. You give me no choice but to –

(**BEAMISH** *appears from the stairwell.*)

**BEAMISH**. Garroway – what in the devil are you doing?

**GARROWAY**. *(Stops.)* Well, sir, I –

**MOLLY**. He's harassing some poor woman in there.

**BEAMISH**. That woman is my fiancée – and she is dressing for dinner.

**GARROWAY**. I'm terribly sorry, Mister Beamish – but, you see, just now I was assaulted by Mister Finch at the Purple Chicken –

**BEAMISH**. That's impossible.

**MOLLY**. George would never do such a thing.

**BEAMISH**. *(A wink to **MOLLY**.)* Besides, George is away on his honeymoon –

**MOLLY**. Or soon will be!

**BEAMISH**. – and, in his absence, he lent my fiancée his sleeping porch.

(*The door to the sleeping porch opens – and* **MADAME EULALIE** *stands there, wearing Fanny's robe and holding her shoes.*)

| MADAME EULALIE. | MOLLY. |
|---|---|
| Hello again. | Hello again. |

**GARROWAY**. But I was just *SITTING ACROSS A TABLE FROM HIM!*

**BEAMISH**. *Delusions*, Garroway. And for an aspiring poet – not altogether bad. Have you heard of Blake? Rimbaud?

**GARROWAY.** But –

**BEAMISH.** What you need, Garroway, is a good glass of whiskey.

**GARROWAY.** But –

> (**BEAMISH** *and* **MADAME EULALIE** *lead* **GARROWAY** *toward the stairwell –)*

**BEAMISH.** I suggest the "Purple Chicken". We'll meet you there.

**GARROWAY.** But –

> (**BEAMISH** *slams the door and* **GARROWAY** *is gone.)*

**BEAMISH.** Don't worry, Molly. George will turn up.

> *(Indicates sleeping porch.)*

In the meantime, why don't you have a little rest? You've had quite the day.

> (**BEAMISH** *and* **MADAME EULALIE** *exit into the apartment, as –)*

> (**MOLLY** *enters –)*

### The Sleeping Porch

> *(She stands, looking around the room – in the exact spot where* **MADAME EULALIE** *stood. What's more: her shoes are identical to those worn by* **MADAME EULALIE**.*)*

**MOLLY.** *(A tired sigh.)* Ahhh...

> *(She sits on the bed and removes her shoes, as –)*

(**FINCH** *pokes his head out and sees only the shoes, exactly as before.*)

**FINCH.**  Oh, May – my dear May Stubbs – you've come back!

(**MOLLY** *freezes in place.*)

I'm so glad it's you. If they were to find me in here, I'd have a lot to answer for –

(*And as* **FINCH** *climbs out from under the bed and stands up, he finds himself eye-to-eye with* **MOLLY**.)

**MOLLY.**  (*Sharp.*) Yes, you do, George.

**FINCH.**  Molly, it's not what you think!

(*Suddenly:* **FANNY** *emerges from one of the two doors of the wardrobe. She is red-faced, breathing hard.*)

**FANNY.**  Enough! I can't do this anymore!

**MOLLY.**  AND HER, TOO?!

**FINCH.**  Molly, no, it's –

**MOLLY.**  (*As she goes.*) IT'S TRUE! IT'S ALL TRUE!

(**MOLLY** *rushes out, as –*)

(**FINCH** *wheels on* **FANNY**.)

**FINCH.**  What are you doing in there?!

(*And now:* **MULLETT** *emerges from the other door of the wardrobe.*)

**MULLETT.**  It's awful hard to have a honeymoon around this place!

**FINCH.**  Mullet?!

**MULLETT.** Isn't your own wedding enough, sir – that you've got to butt in on mine?!

**FINCH.** My wedding was ruined.

**MULLETT.** Ruined how?

**FINCH.** By HER.

**FANNY.** ME?

**MULLETT.** FANNY?

**FANNY.** *(Instantly, as before.)* DON'T TURN ME OVER TO THE BULLS, MISTER! I ONLY DID IT FOR MY DEAR OLD –

**MULLETT.** OKAY, FANNY: what have you done?

**FANNY.** It was a little something that just *fell in my lap.*

**MULLETT.** Hand it over. Whatever it is.

>   *(And **FANNY** produces the pearl necklace.)*

**FINCH.** Molly's necklace!

**MULLETT.** I'm sorry, Mister Finch.

>   *(**MULLETT** gives the necklace to **FINCH**.)*

**FANNY.** But, Pookee...

**MULLETT.** From now on, sir, we are duck farmers.

**FINCH.** My very best to you both. I need to find Molly.

>   *(**MULLETT** nods, happily – as he and **FANNY** follow **FINCH** out of the sleeping porch and across –)*

## The Roof.

**MULLETT.** Fanny, we are now officially retired.

**FANNY.** Except for the occasional visit to Macy's.

**MULLETT.** Well, sure, around the *holidays*.

(*– And into the apartment, as –*)

(**GARROWAY** *opens the stairwell door, at the same moment that –*)

(**FERRIS** *emerges from the fire escape.*)

**FERRIS.** Hello again, bobby.

**GARROWAY.** Once and for all, *my name is not –*

**FERRIS.** I'm looking for a Mister George Finch.

**GARROWAY.** Well, get in line, pal – cause SO AM I!

(**MRS. WADDINGTON** *now emerges from the fire escape –*)

**MRS. WADDINGTON.** Ferris, there you are! Finch is hiding in the sleeping porch!

**FERRIS.** I couldn't have *written it* any better!

(**MRS. WADDINGTON** *sees* **GARROWAY**.)

**GARROWAY.** YOU!

**MRS. WADDINGTON.** YIKES!

**GARROWAY.** PINCHED!

(**MRS. WADDINGTON** *rushes into the sleeping porch, just as –*)

(**FINCH** *emerges from the apartment and sees* **GARROWAY** –)

**FINCH.** YIKES.

**GARROWAY.** (*Sees* **FINCH**.) YOU.

**FINCH.** WAIT.

**GARROWAY.** STOP.

> (**SIGSBEE** *appears from the stairwell.*)

**SIGSBEE.** *(Sees* **FINCH.***)* PINCH!

**GARROWAY.** *(Sees* **SIGSBEE.***)* YOU.

**SIGSBEE.** *(Sees* **GARROWAY.***)* YOU!

**GARROWAY.** STOP!

**SIGSBEE.** YES!

**GARROWAY.** *(To* **FERRIS.***)* YOU.

**FERRIS.** SIR?

**GARROWAY.** *(Pointing to the sleeping porch door.)* GUARD.

**FERRIS.** RIGHT.

**GARROWAY.** *(Putting his hat on* **FERRIS'** *head.)* DEPUTY!

**FERRIS.** BOBBY!

**GARROWAY.** *DON'T CALL ME BOBBY!!!* MY NAME IS –

**SIGSBEE.** *(It comes to him.) GARROWAY!!!* THAT'S IT! GARROWAY, GARROWAY, WHAT A BEAUTIFUL NAME!

**GARROWAY.** *(To* **SIGSBEE.***)* I want my money back!

**SIGSBEE.** And I want to give it to you!

**GARROWAY.** You *do?*

**SIGSBEE.** All I need in return is that *worthless stock certificate* I gave you by mistake.

**GARROWAY.** With pleasure!

> (**SIGSBEE** *and* **GARROWAY** *make their exchange, as –)*

(**MRS. WADDINGTON** *begins pounding on the door of the sleeping porch.*)

**VOICE OF MRS. WADDINGTON.** Ferris – open the door!

**FERRIS.** I'm afraid I can't do that, Madame. I've been deputized.

**VOICE OF MRS. WADDINGTON.** You're going to be EUTHANIZED if you don't open this door!

**FERRIS.** I'm an Officer of the Law. Simply following orders.

**VOICE OF MRS. WADDINGTON.** Ferris, you are NO LONGER IN MY EMPLOYMENT.

**FERRIS.** *Thank you*, Madame.

**FINCH.** Mister Waddington – I've recovered Molly's necklace.

(*He lifts the pearl necklace.*)

Apparently, it was stolen at the wedding.

**SIGSBEE.** Good job, Winch. Give it here.

**FINCH.** I thought I'd give it to Molly myself.

(**SIGSBEE** *grabs the necklace.*)

**SIGSBEE.** You'll do *no such thing*. I'm the head of the family now – and I'm gonna have this necklace RESET. With even FINER PEARLS!

**FINCH.** That's *right good* of you, sir.

(**SIGSBEE** *puts his arm around* **FINCH.**)

**SIGSBEE.** You ain't seen nothin', yet.

**GARROWAY.** Hold it right there!

(*Approaching* **FINCH.**)

You and me've got our own score to settle, Mister Finch.

(**BEAMISH** *and* **MADAME EULALIE** *emerge from the stairwell.*)

**BEAMISH.** That would be "you and I", Garroway.

**GARROWAY.** *(Re:* **FINCH.***)* This man pummeled me with a pasta plate!

**BEAMISH.** All a terrible misunderstanding, I'm sure.

**GARROWAY.** And that woman in there attacked me with a pepper-pot!

**BEAMISH.** What woman?

**VOICE OF MRS. WADDINGTON.** *(Pounding on the door.)* LET ME OUT OF HERE THIS INSTANT!

**FERRIS.** *(Proudly.)* Mrs. Waddington, sir.

**SIGSBEE.** *(Happily, to* **GARROWAY.***)* I'll handle this, Carradine!

(**SIGSBEE** *stands just outside the closed door of the sleeping porch.*)

**VOICE OF MRS. WADDINGTON.** Sigsbee! – I can explain *everything!*

**SIGSBEE.** Yeah, well, SO CAN I. The reason for all this conniving and canoodling is that we're stuck *living in the East.* But NOT ANY MORE. I'm a wealthy man again and YOU KNOW WHAT THAT MEANS!

(*He opens the door...and* **MRS. WADDINGTON** *peeks her head out.*)

**MRS. WADDINGTON.** You *wouldn't...*

**SIGSBEE.** Lace up your knickers, Nellie – I'm takin' you to the Wild West!

**MRS. WADDINGTON.** Sigsbee – *under no circumstances will I –*

**SIGSBEE.** Tie a can to it, lady! I'm the Big Noise, now – I'm the LAW ROUND THESE PARTS.

> (**MRS. WADDINGTON** *steps out of the sleeping porch, as –)*

> (**MULLETT** *and* **FANNY** *emerge from the apartment.)*

> *(They are in "duck farming clothes."* **MULLETT** *carries a suitcase.* **FANNY** *carries a box with a colorful ribbon.)*

**MULLETT.** Well, we're off.

> *(Blows a quick duck call.)*

The ducks are waiting!

**FANNY.** Mister Waddington – the store on the corner just sent this up.

**SIGSBEE.** Ah, perfect.

> *(As* **SIGSBEE** *sings, he reaches into the box and removes...*.*)*

*WHERE THE AIR IS SO PURE AND THE ZEPHYRS SO FREE*
*AND THE BREEZES SO BALMY AND LIGHT*

> *(... A large, bright pink cowboy hat.* **SIGSBEE** *approaches* **MRS. WADDINGTON.***)*

**MRS. WADDINGTON.** *Oh, no...*

**SIGSBEE.**

*OH I WOULD NOT EXCHANGE MY OLD HOME ON THE RANGE*

---

* A license to produce *Over the Moon* does not include a performance license for any third-party or copyrighted music. Licensees should create an original composition or use music in the public domain. For further information, please see the Music and Third-Party Materials Use Note on page iii.

**MRS. WADDINGTON.** *You wouldn't dare...*

**SIGSBEE.**

*FOR ALL OF YOUR CITIES SO BRIGHT*

> (**SIGSBEE** *places the cowboy hat on her head.*
> *He looks at her with pride.*)

Wheee...

**MRS. WADDINGTON.** *(Through clenched teeth)* ...Doggies.

> *(It is now night. A huge, full moon looms*
> *above and behind them all.)*

> (**MOLLY** *enters from the stairwell. Everyone*
> *turns to her.*)

**MOLLY.** *(Bitter.)* Well. Look at all the happy couples.

**BEAMISH.** Molly, I assure you, there is a completely logical explan –

**MOLLY.** I want to hear it from George.

> *(Everyone turns to* **FINCH.**)

Well?

**FINCH.** Yes?

**MOLLY.** *(Re:* **FANNY.**) What about *her?*

**FINCH.** That woman is a thief.

**MULLETT.** The best in the business.

**FANNY.** Now retired.

**FINCH.** She stole your pearl necklace –

**SIGSBEE.** At my request –

**MRS. WADDINGTON.** What?!

**SIGSBEE.** *(To* **MOLLY.**) – so I could have the pearls reset for *you.*

**FINCH.** Isn't that nice?

**MOLLY.** *(Not yet swayed, re:* **MADAME EULALIE.***)* And what about her?

**FINCH.** All in the past!

**MADAME EULALIE.** And when I gaze into George's future, Molly – the only woman I see there is *you.*

  *(To* **FINCH.***)*

Tell her, George. *It's now or never.*

  *(Everyone turns to face* **FINCH.***)*

**FINCH.** *Ummmmmmmm...*

**BEAMISH.** What I believe George is trying to say –

**FINCH.** I'll handle this, Jimmy.

  *(To* **MOLLY,** *from his heart.)*

The woman I adore, Molly...the *only woman I adore...* is you.

**MOLLY.** I want to believe you, George – I do – but when I saw all these women up here –

**FINCH.** Oh, I have women up here all the time.

**MULLETT.** *(Helpfully.)* And they're all *nude.*

**MOLLY.** They're *what?!*

**FINCH.** I'm a PAINTER, Molly. These women *pose for me.*

**MOLLY.** Well, George: I'll have to ask you to never paint another picture.

**ALL (BUT MOLLY & FINCH).** *(As it suits them.)* HOORAY! / THAT'S GREAT! / FINALLY.

**FINCH.** I'll do whatever you ask, Molly. Only say you'll marry me tomorrow.

**MOLLY.** No, George. I'll marry you *tonight*.

**ALL (BUT MRS. WADDINGTON).** HOORAY! / WONDERFUL! / BRAVO! / HUP-HIP-HOODELEE-DOO!

**FINCH.** Do you mean it?!

**MOLLY.** The minister from Flushing is right downstairs! – dining at the Purple Chicken!

**FINCH.** Now, *that's* a clergyman!

(**FINCH** *and* **MOLLY** *kiss.*)

**BEAMISH.** Maybe he'll do a TWO for ONE!

(**BEAMISH** *and* **MADAME EULALIE** *kiss.*)

**MULLETT.** Maybe we'll have a reception after all!

(**MULLETT** *and* **FANNY** *kiss.*)

**SIGSBEE.** Oh, rooty-tooty, I'm feelin' *young again!*

(**SIGSBEE** *starts to kiss* **MRS. WADDINGTON**, *but she stops him –*)

**MRS. WADDINGTON.** *Not so fast, cowboy.* I still want some proof that Mister Finch can support our dear Molly.

(**BEAMISH** *quickly whispers something in* **MRS. WADDINGTON**'s *ear.*)

*(Fully changed.)* You don't *say?!* Well – that is music to my ears. I always knew you were the man for her, George.

| **FINCH.** | **MOLLY.** |
|---|---|
| Thank you, Mother. | See there! |

**MRS. WADDINGTON.** Imagine, Ferris, if any of this would have ended up in the *Tattler*.

**FERRIS.** *(A wry smile.)* The mind *reels*.

**FINCH.** Let's find that man from Flushing!

**GARROWAY.** *Just a minute.* There still remains the matter of various pasta plate and pepper-pot assaults!

**BEAMISH.** Garroway, do you know where the soul of a true poet is born?

**GARROWAY.** Ireland, sir?

**BEAMISH.** In *suffering.* These reckless and wild events will surely *fire the kiln of your creative soul.* Now, get to work.

**GARROWAY.** But my notebook, sir – I can't find it.

**BEAMISH.** It will turn up.

**MRS. WADDINGTON.** Ferris, we'll need a table for eight.

**FERRIS.** Thank you, Madame, but I believe you terminated my employment. I shall be striking out on my own.

**MRS. WADDINGTON.** Well, should you need me to *put in a word for you* –

**FERRIS.** You've already put in more words than you know. Cheerio!

    (**FERRIS** *exits through the apartment.*)

**BEAMISH.** *(Grandly, to them* **ALL**.*)* Shall we?

**FINCH.** After you, Mister Showers.

**SIGSBEE.** Everybody now!

    (*And they* **ALL** *begin to sing, as they exit down the stairwell in the following order:* **SIGSBEE** *and* **MRS. WADDINGTON;** **BEAMISH**

and **MADAME EULALIE; FINCH** and **MOLLY;**
and, finally, **MULLETT** and **FANNY.**\*)

**ALL (BUT GARROWAY).**
HOME, HOME ON THE RANGE
WHERE THE DEER AND THE ANTELOPE PLAY

**FINCH.** Mullett – grab my ukulele!

**MULLETT.** Yes, sir!

**ALL (BUT GARROWAY).**
WHERE SELDOM IS HEARD A DISCOURAGING WORD
AND THE SKIES ARE NOT CLOUDY ALL DAY

(**MULLETT** has grabbed a ukulele from inside
the apartment.)

(As he and **FANNY** are leaving, **FANNY** bumps
headlong into **GARROWAY** –)

**GARROWAY.** Sorry, Miss.

**FANNY.** Have a good night!

(As **GARROWAY** steps to the edge of the roof,
downstage, he pats his chest pocket...and
discovers his notebook. He looks quickly to
the stairwell door, where –)

(**FANNY** gives him a friendly little wink, and
is gone.)

(**GARROWAY** opens his notebook. Reads.)

**GARROWAY.** The story is told both night and noon

of brutal streets where hearts are strewn

---

\* A license to produce Over the Moon does not include a performance
license for any third-party or copyrighted music. Licensees should create
an original composition or use music in the public domain. For further
information, please see the Music and Third-Party Materials Use Note
on page iii.

**GARROWAY.** But from the gales of love's monsoon

A sudden rainbow does festoon
Each new-found couple here aswoon
Beneath the Sun and over the Moon.

*(He turns and looks at the moon, as the –)*

*(Lights fade.)*

## End of Play

www.ingramcontent.com/pod-product-compliance
Lightning Source LLC
Chambersburg PA
CBHW070330120726
47909CB00008B/2671